UNBOUND III

GOODBYE EARTH

CAROLINE FURLONG   GRANT SKELTON

ROB ROWNTREE   ROBIN POND   DAVE STEINMAN

STEVEN FRITZ   N L SWEENEY

SHARON KAE REAMER   A A JANKIEWICZ

DOUGLAS OWEN

Science Fiction and Fantasy Publications

UNBOUND III : GOODBYE EARTH

Science Fiction and Fantasy Publications

https://scififantasypublications.com
An imprint of DAOwen Publications

Unbound III: Goodbye Earth
Edited by Douglas Owen

ISBN 978-1-928094-55-5
EISBN 978-1-928094-56-2

Jacket art: MMT Productions
10 9 8 7 6 5 4 3 2 1

A WORD FROM THE EDITOR

The Unbound Anthology is a project I'm happy to publish every couple of years. The manuscripts contained in each edition are new and never before published works from various authors around the world.

As the editor, I always look for wonderful stories when reviewing the submissions. Not all of the works submitted can be printed though, which is a shame for many amazingly talented authors submit to us. No, we pick those stories that pique our interest or make us think. Even when they are reviewed, the names of the authors are kept back to ensure recognition is not a factor.

Many talented authors have taken the time to write and rewrite for your enjoyment. So please take a comfortable seat, your favourite drink, and curl up to the inner thoughts of the writers in this edition of Unbound.

CAROLINE FURLONG

A sci-fi/fantasy writer, Caroline Furlong lives in Virginia, U.S.A. Her novelette "Halcyon" was the cover story for Cirsova Magazine's Summer Special, which is available for purchase through Amazon. She won Honorable Mention in the Writers of the Future Contest for her work on two separate occasions. She enjoys history, classic cars, swimming and - of course - reading and writing. For more information, please visit her at www.carolinefurlong.wordpress.com.

ALL THE LAMPS ARE LIT

BY CAROL FURLONG

It's been several years since I quit nursing. I didn't quit because I hated the work – far from it. It's impossible to hate working with kids who have terminal cancer. Sure, you hate the cancer, but you can't hate the kids.

No, I quit because I got married, had kids of my own, and landed a career as a writer of all things. But that's beginning the story at the ending.

I still remember it like it was yesterday. Just out of nursing school, I was bright-eyed and determined to help some people – kids mostly. Maybe it was an early manifestation of maternal instincts that led to my desire to care for them. It certainly wasn't due to poor parenting. My mother and father were the best in the business. Whatever the reason was, I managed to end up at a hospital for terminally ill kids.

That's where I met Shawnee.

She was sixteen when I met her, and not bald. They had discovered she had cancer when she was twelve, meaning that she had lived the last four years of her life in the hospital. Though they kept testing her and doing their best to treat her disease, the doctors knew they would never find a cure in time for her. Eventually, her mom and dad figured it out, too.

Shawnee already knew the cancer was going to take her. She had known for three years – at least, that's what she said when I asked. It was like hearing the warning whistle before the train pulls up to the station, she told me. You know it is coming, you know you're going on it, but you can't see it yet.

The first day I walked into her hospital room, I wasn't sure what to make of it. The lights were dimmed and the window blinds were drawn, so part of my problem was letting my eyes adjust to the darkness. In the rest of the hospital, the lights were all on. Looking into her room was like looking into the mouth of the Cave of Wonders from *One Thousand and One Arabian Nights*.

I thought at first that my little patient was sound asleep or didn't want visitors and turned to leave. But just as I did, a little girl's voice spoke from the void. "You can come in, Nurse. I'm not asleep yet."

She turned the lights up as I swung around to face her. The sight of her room made me jump back in shock.

Her room was not a neat, white-walled, pristine cell like all the other hospital rooms. Even when the kids were allowed to add some personal touches they never looked like this. Some part of me thought my eyes were playing tricks, that I was seeing things.

From the ceiling of Shawnee's room hung model starships and even planets. Everything from the U. S. S. *Voyager* to what I recognized as a NASA shuttlecraft dangled there. They rotated sedately in place, like fish swimming at the top of a tank. There was only one empty space in the school of flying models, and it was right above the head of her bed.

And the walls! You would have thought a theater had thrown up in her room. The walls were plastered with movie posters placed so close together you couldn't see any paint showing between them. The ones I noticed right off were from *Star Wars*, but later recognized some *Titan A. E.* and *John Carter* pictures pinned up as well.

Every spare piece of furniture had action figures and toys spilling off of it. It looked like all of my geeky cousin's toy boxes had been transported to the hospital, the items dumped out, sorted through, and arranged artfully around the room. But instead of the familiar zombies, cadavers, witches, ogres, and whatnot, Shawnee's decoration theme was aimed skyward, with superheroes and flying aliens – and, yes, more spaceships.

"What?" I managed at last.

"They weren't all mine to begin with." The girl giggled at my surprise. "The doctors and nurses keep bringing them to me. I tell some of them that I don't need toys and they say they know, but they still keep giving them to me. There are others I don't tell to stop, because I know that they feel better giving me things. If I were to say, 'Please, I don't need it' to those poor souls, they would break down and cry right in front of me. I'd rather they brought me treasures instead of tears, for their sakes."

As she spoke I turned to look at her. She was a slim black girl who looked thirteen, not sixteen. Her hair was cut short around her face. Despite her treatments and the cancer, you wouldn't know she was sick by looking at her. She wasn't emaciated or hollow-eyed, not yet anyway. And her mind was sharp as a tack, you could see it in her posture. She didn't slump in the bed but sat up straight and alert.

Her warm brown eyes scanned the items around her room lovingly before turning back to me. "I'm Shawnee. What's your name?"

"Deirdre." I crossed the threshold, careful to look out for toys the unwary could step on. "I'm sorry, it just startled me." I gestured toward the ceiling. That was when I noticed there was a model X-Wing amidst the action figures on the table beside her bed.

"It startles most people the first time," she said, smiling again. "Sometimes even my parents seem shocked to see all the posters and toys. They say they have no idea where they'll put them when it's time for me to go home."

I was to learn later she didn't mean when her parents took her home, but when she was gone and they had to clean out the room.

But at the time I just nodded and went to check her chart. That was when I saw she held something in her hands. It looked like a mechanical cat, with blue armor instead of fur and gears where the joints met. "That's a nice Voltron toy you have there."

She threw back her head and laughed. It was a sweet laugh, crystal clear and pure as a bird's song. "It's not a Voltron, though you're right, it is Japanese. This is my toy Shield Liger. He's a zoid."

"Never heard of it," I admitted. Finished with the chart, I sat on the end of her bed and eyed the little machine. It didn't have eyes, but it definitely stared back at me. I got the impression it either considered me to be harmless or amusing, neither of which exactly helped my pride. "Does he like to be petted?"

She leaned forward and held the toy out to me with her right hand. With her left, she pointed to its chin. "You can rub him here. He likes that."

With my finger, I reached out and gently scratched the toy's plastic jaw. Shawnee did a good imitation of a cat purring, and then we both fell back from each other, giggling. "You're new here, aren't you, Deirdre?"

"Yes, I am." I did a more thorough scan of the room. "Wow, you have a lot of posters. And I've never seen so many models. Do you want to be a pilot when you grow up?"

She shook her head. "No." She looked down at the toy in her hands. "I'm not going to grow up, Deirdre."

Her flat statement shocked me. Most kids don't talk about dying of cancer until they're almost ready to go. They get down in the dumps, of course – who wouldn't? But usually death was a taboo subject in the ward. Not until just before they died were we supposed to admit there was no hope.

Before I could say anything to comfort or allay her worries, she looked back at me and met my eyes. They were brown, as I had known they would be, but a brown flecked with hints of gold. Shawnee was no ordinary child – nor was she an ordinary cancer patient. Her body was on the ground and failing her, but her mind and soul were *flying*.

The moment passed when she started speaking again. "Besides, I wouldn't want to be a pilot if I could only fly a plane. I'd rather pilot a starship – or a zoid." She cuddled the toy gently to her chest.

"What's wrong with flying planes?" I asked. My brain seemed stuck in one gear; first the room, now this strange girl. She was more grown up than anyone I knew. Cancer kids, they're always more adult than regular kids. They have to be. But Shawnee was more mature than any young patient I had cared for since I started nursing.

"They only fly around Earth." Shawnee pointed to a model hanging from the ceiling on her left. It was Captain Kirk's *Enterprise*. "Starships can go *anywhere*. Tatooine, Kashyyyk, Zi, Vulcan…"

"Deneb IV, Endor, and…" I tried to think of another planet, but none came to mind.

Shawnee nodded eagerly. "That's right. I don't want to stay on Earth, I want to go all over the place." Setting the toy down in her lap, she gestured expansively to encompass all the pictures, models, and toys in the room. "I want to go to all these places and more. I want to go everywhere and do everything. You can't smuggle spice through Paris, or meet Trofts in Atlanta, or learn logic in Cairo. Not the kind Spock uses, anyway." She giggled again.

That's how it started. The two of us got to know each other through pop culture. I soon learned Shawnee had an almost encyclopedic knowledge of several dozen different stories, from the well-known *Star Wars* and *Star Trek* brands down to the lesser known *Zoids* and *Thundercats* franchises.

You would think this fascination with pop culture would rot her brain. But it didn't. It *couldn't*. Not long after chatting with Shawnee, I met her doctor. He told me not only her condition, but the girl had a genius IQ. By the time I met Shawnee, she had two Ph.D.s and was working on another one.

No wonder she seemed so grown-up. Physically she was sixteen, but her mind was the mind of a twenty-two-year-old. She had lived more life through her brain than she had in her body.

I met her mother and father later that day. Her mother wore a business suit and pearls that gleamed like snowdrops against her mahogany skin. Shawnee's father worked at a nearby military base. He cut quite a figure even in his casual Air Force uniform, with his hair cropped close to his skull and his wide, bright smile. When I saw him, I couldn't help but say, "So *you're* the one who taught Shawnee to love flying!"

He laughed and shook his head. "No, I didn't. Shawnee was a pilot before she was born. She came into the world on a cloud."

"Or straight from the stars," her mother said, smiling. But there was sadness in her face, as though she knew what was coming for her precious daughter. I looked them over again more carefully, seeing for the first time the worry lines in their faces. They both knew she was dying. "My daughter received her gifts straight from heaven, Nurse. There's very little of either of us in her," Shawnee's mother added.

"She would beg to differ," I said.

"I know she does," her mother agreed. "But it's the truth. She was meant for the stars, not little old Earth. It can't hold her for much longer."

Her hand sought her husband's instinctively and he clutched it, as though he were fighting a sudden gust of wind that threatened to tear the controls of his plane from his grip. I had never seen parents so heartbroken and yet so proud of their dying child. They knew they were losing her. But they were proud of her nonetheless.

We went to her room not long after that. Shawnee's parents would have doted on her, I think, except for the fact she spoke to them like a twenty-two-year-old instead of a sixteen-year-old. They treated her as though she was a doll made of fine porcelain. Except this doll could reach out and take their hands and pull them into tight embraces that turned knuckles white.

Day after day I made special trips to visit Shawnee. She'd be playing with her toys, or studying from a big book of mathematics, or submitting with the patience of a saint to another test. One day, I caught her writing in a little notebook.

I was supposed to be at the other end of the hospital, but couldn't avoid stopping by Shawnee's room on the way to look in on her. We'd developed quite a friendship by that point; I was beginning to consider her a little sister. Every morning I came in for work I would stop by her room, if only to glance inside and see what she was doing.

This was supposed to be a glance moment, but Shawnee saw me and waved me in. Biting my lip, worrying what my boss was going to say, I stepped into her room. But Shawnee made it quick. "Deirdre, I need to talk to you later. Is that okay?"

"Why sure, sweetheart," I said, startled. "I may be busy all day, but I'll stop by before I go off shift. Is that all right?"

"Yes, I should be ready by then." And Shawnee went back to writing.

I looked at her. She still seemed perfectly healthy, but there was a tightness in her eyes, as if she were worried about something. That in itself was surprising. Shawnee had never shown worry about anything while I had known her.

While jogging up and down halls, administering needles, cuddling kids, and doing paperwork I pondered that look on her face. It was during lunch that I guessed why Shawnee looked worried. I nearly choked on my sandwich when I did.

Somehow, someway, she knew her time was coming up. She knew she was going to die, not on some amorphous, future date, but sometime in the near future. The realization hit me like a punch in the stomach.

Once I was officially off shift, I hurried down to Shawnee's room.

No one else was there. Shawnee's Shield Liger sat on her lap. I had never seen him out of her reach. It was like he was her special talisman or guardian angel – as long as she could touch him, she was safe. For the first time, I wondered what would happen to him when she died.

She stroked his head as I came in. "Deirdre, I need you to do something for me."

"Anything, sweetie," I promised.

She shook her head. "No, don't say that. You don't know what I'm going to ask. I'd do it myself, but I haven't got the time. I know I don't. Neither do my father or my mother. They've got to work so they can take care of my brothers."

"Brothers?" I asked, confused. She was an only child.

A slight smile touched her lips. "They don't know it yet, but they're going to have a couple more kids by this time next year." She pointed to a stack of journals on the table next to her bed. An envelope and two thumb drives sat on top of the pile. "Can you run an errand for me, Deirdre? These need to go to my cousin. He works at Houghton Mifflin."

"Sure, Sweetie," I said again. Taking the books from her side table, I put the drives in my pocket. "What are they?"

For a moment, Shawnee studied me closely, her fingers tracing the

Shield Liger's head. "Deirdre, I'm going to tell you a secret. You can't tell anyone else, not even my parents. They should only know after I'm gone."

Tears sprang to my eyes. "Oh, Shawnee…!"

"No, Deirdre, don't say it. We both know there's no cure for me." She handed me a tissue and I wiped my eyes, trying to stuff my feelings in a box somewhere in my chest. It worked – partially. I stopped crying, but my hands still shook.

She smiled again. "I love you too, Deirdre. You're the big sister I never had. But the thing is that I am dying, and you've got to accept it. As for the books" – she gestured at the stack in my lap – "I can't ask my parents to take them to Shane. They're not strong enough to ferry these books to him. I'm afraid they might throw them away for the same reason you're trying not to cry. I don't expect you or them not to cry when I'm gone, but these have to be delivered safely. Shane's strong, like you, and he can take care of them." She gave me the directions to the Houghton Mifflin building.

"Okay, but what are they, Shawnee?" I asked.

Leaning back in her bed, Shawnee closed her eyes. "Books, Deirdre. Books I wrote myself. Some are science books I'm hoping will finally get us into deep space. It'll take a lot of money and time, but I know we'll get there sooner or later."

I stared at her, openmouthed. She must have sensed by my silence that I was flabbergasted, because she smiled. "I just got my third Ph.D. last week," she said. "There will be people who will say I'm wrong, or stupid, or a dreamer. People who want to rule the world rather than find new ones to explore."

"But that's okay, Deirdre." She opened her eyes and looked at me. It was like looking into the eyes of a lioness. "It's okay, because they're wrong. They've chosen the darkness of ignorance and selfishness, and they're going to lose in the end because of that. These books…" She tapped the one on the top. It had a fuzzy pink cover and a tortoiseshell kitten on it. "These books have the answers to space travel. I know they'll help us get to at least three solar systems besides this one, maybe even the next five systems. After that –" she smiled – "the sky's the limit.

"The rest are fiction novels." She laughed as I smiled weakly. "I know. I had only intended to write the science books, but I couldn't help branching out. They'll be published under different names for a few years. Most are my own stories, but you'll see some new Marvel, DC, Star Trek, and Star Wars material that will eventually have my name on it. I've written for a few other franchises, too. Shane can keep you in the loop on how they do. He's my agent for these and the other stories." She put her head back again and closed her eyes.

I looked down at the books in my lap, feeling as if they had suddenly metamorphosed from mass-produced journals made in China into jewel encrusted manuscripts from Ancient Alexandria. It was another few minutes before I found my voice. "How long have you been doing this?"

"I've been writing down my discoveries since I was seven. When I was diagnosed with cancer at twelve, I moved into fiction."

"Why?"

"Because fiction drives our dreams, Deirdre. It helps us expand our minds. It shows us a world in a grain of sand, an ocean in a raindrop, or a forest in a flower. It draws us to other people and puts us in touch with eternity, takes us out of ourselves and out of time and space." She sighed. "Without fiction, life is drab. It's a mill, a mill that small-minded people can use to beat us down and make us nothing but ants in a farm or animals without a purpose. We're neither."

A wave of wonder and sorrow washed through me as I stared at her. This marvelous young child had put into words something I had felt since I was her age but had never been able to describe.

My hands clenched into fists as anger boiled up in me, born out of my sorrow. It wasn't fair. This girl was brilliant, with so much to give to the world. But she would never get the chance, thanks to the cancer destroying her body. It wasn't *fair!*

Shawnee smiled again, as if reading my mind. "'Since when is life fair?'" she quoted, doing her best imitation of Peter Falk in *The Princess Bride*. "'Where is that written?'"

I shook my head too overcome by my feelings. She laughed again. "I've already published quite a bit of fiction, Deirdre," she murmured, opening her eyes and looking at me. "I needed the Ph.D.s to get the science published. Otherwise, the scientific community wouldn't give me the time of day. They're a stubborn, arrogant bunch."

Her smile widened to an angelic degree. "We're all here for different reasons and different times, Deirdre. My time and my mission in this world is almost done. I only have a little more work to do, and then I'll be ready to go. If Shane wasn't working so much now he could drop by to pick up the manuscripts, but he's got too much on his plate. I need someone to take them to him. Could you do that for me, Deirdre? Please?"

"I'll be happy to, Shawnee." Leaning over, I kissed her on the forehead. "And I'll ask him for an advance copy of whichever one gets published first."

"You'd better make it clear you want an advance copy of the stories," she said. "Unless you have a degree in physics or quantum mechanics stashed up your sleeve somewhere?"

"I barely got through calculus!" I laughed. "But I'll read the fiction, I promise."

As I stood up she reached out and grasped my wrist. "You're here for a reason, too, Deirdre," she whispered. "You're special. You're going to have a long life, and I want you to use it well. You understand?"

I pulled free of her grip and took her hand. "I will, I promise." As I squeezed her hand, the toy in her lap caught my eye, and I got my hundredth shock of the afternoon. "Shawnee..." I gasped, staring at it in disbelief.

"Shhh!" She gave my hand another, confidential squeeze. "There are more things in Heaven and Earth than are dreamt of in man's philosophies, Deirdre – many, many more things. Now hurry! Mom and Dad will be here soon, and they can't see you with those." Giving my hand one last squeeze, she let me go.

Somehow, I stumbled out of the hospital to my car. I put the books carefully in the front passenger seat and pulled my car keys from my purse. I got them in the ignition just before the tears started.

Shawnee was right. I did consider her a sister, more than she knew. My parents had never had other children; I was an only child, just like she was, or had been. And to lose her now, when I still barely knew her...

That was most of my reason for leaning on the steering wheel, crying so hard I could barely breathe. But there was another reason, too. Before leaving the room, I had seen the toy on Shawnee's lap *move*.

It hadn't been a stiff movement either. The way the toy was designed, it couldn't move like a real cat, the way most robots can't do more than jerkily mimic human movements. It couldn't lift or turn its head, couldn't wag its tail, or snuggle closer to Shawnee. It was battery operated and, unless she wanted to break it, Shawnee couldn't move its legs herself. At least, that was the way it was supposed to work.

But the way the toy moved when I saw it, it acted *alive*. No battery could make its head turn, and yet the toy's head *had* turned. Its legs weren't supposed to move without a switch between its hips being flipped. But the toy had pulled its forelegs to its chest and nuzzled Shawnee like an actual cat. And I *knew* the switch had been in the *off* position.

It was too much in too short a time – Shawnee's impending death, her secret life as an author and groundbreaking scientist, the toy's inexplicable movement – so much sad, astonishing news delivered to me in the space of an hour.

Finally, I managed to pull myself together so that I could function. I started the car, then drove all the way to the Houghton Mifflin building. Finding a place to park, I managed to get in touch with Shawnee's cousin and he let me inside.

Shane was a handsome young man, about my age, with bright eyes and a sincere smile. He wore a wedding ring on his left hand and there was a scar along his chin that stood out against his dark complexion. When I saw a picture on his desk of him in uniform with several other soldiers, I guessed he'd earned his scar in combat somewhere in the Middle East.

I explained I worked at the hospital where Shawnee was and that she had entrusted the manuscripts to me. It took everything I had not to break down into tears again as I handed over the notebooks, the letter, and fumbled the thumb drives from my pocket. My eyes grew watery, though, and the room started to blurr as I spoke.

He handed me a tissue. "Thank you for bringing these to me,

Miss Callahan." He spoke low and soft, but there was the ring of authority in his voice. "I've been meaning to visit Shawnee, but my wife and I are expecting our first child. Between that and my increased duties here..." He sighed. "I haven't been able to find the time."

I nodded. "Shawnee said that. She understands that you can't make it."

"I know. Logically, reasonably, I know that. But –" He looked away from me and sighed again. "But I still feel like a rat for not visiting her." He turned his gaze back, studying me long and hard. "She must trust you very much to ask you to take care of her books. She won't even give them to her parents."

Blinking hard, I nodded again. "She told me. She's a..." I hiccupped and pretended to cough to cover it up. "She's a very, very special girl," I went on. "You're lucky to be related to her."

"I know," he said, smiling. "What do you think of her room?"

"It was a shock when I saw it first!" I laughed, glad of the change of subject. It helped me get myself back under control. "I've got a cousin who is into some of the same things she likes, but his room is a wax museum of horrors. Hers is different. You walk inside and feel like anything is possible – anything at all." I suddenly remembered the movement of her toy Shield Liger. Had I imagined it, or had it actually happened? It shouldn't have been possible...

But the more I thought about it, the more I believed what I had seen was real. That toy had moved of its own volition. Shawnee hadn't touched it. The toy had moved like a living thing. In some mysterious way, it was actually *alive*.

"Her stories will have the same effect on you, I promise," Shane said, interrupting my thoughts. He didn't seem to notice my mind had wandered. "If you'd like, I'll send you some advance copies of her latest novels. By the way, does she still have Victor?"

I frowned. "Victor?"

He laughed. "There was this mechanical toy cat I gave her –"

"Oh, wait, you mean her Shield Liger?"

"Yes, that's the one. I bought it for her when I was stationed in Okinawa. She was six at the time. I'd watched the television series during high school and introduced her to it a year or two before I gave her the model. She named it Victor."

"She still has him," I said. "He's never out of her reach. I didn't hear his name before, that's all." I wondered if I should tell him what I had seen earlier. Shawnee trusted him...but did she trust him that far?

After a moment's thought, I said, "He's very special to her."

Shane looked at me, his expression abruptly serious. "He's *very* special," he agreed softly. "Did she ever let you pet him?"

"I've given him a scratch or two," I answered, watching his eyes carefully.

He held my gaze for a long moment. "Well, then," he murmured. "I think you know what I mean when I say he's not your average...toy."

A thrill ran through my veins. "No, he's far from average," I agreed.

Slowly, Shane nodded. "And I *would* like an advance copy of Shawnee's latest novel," I added. "I'll be happy to pay for it, and the novels published in the future. I'm not much of a scientist, I'm afraid. I wouldn't understand any of those books." I blushed as I spoke.

"Neither am I, but one of the guys I knew in the Army raves about Shawnee's scientific works." Shane laughed. "He's running for Congress in the hopes of getting NASA to use her discoveries to make better ships."

"I hope he succeeds – for her," I said.

"So do I." Shane reached down, opened a drawer in his desk, and pulled out a book. "Compliments of the house," he said, holding it out to me. "Not all advance copies are bought. Some are given free so that the author gets better press." He smiled at me again. "Shawnee would prefer it this way."

I took the book and put it in my purse. "Thank you." We shook hands and I left.

When I crawled into bed that night, I could feel the heartache ripping through my chest. I had been crying on and off since I got home. Desperate for something that would ease the pain, I took the book Shane gave me and started to read.

Usually, I'm a poor reader. I can write well – in school, my English marks were all high. But to get through a book I had to schedule reading time for it. I couldn't read for more than an hour without eventually losing interest in the words on the page. So when I got into bed with Shawnee's book, I had not intended to read beyond eight o'clock.

But by the time I put the book down, it was midnight.

For a few minutes after finishing the story I sat in bed, staring at the opposite wall. I had known Shawnee was a brilliant, wonderful girl. But while reading this book, I learned that I barely knew her. The novel was fantasy, not science fiction, as I would have expected. It was full of derring-do with a touch of romance, but that wasn't what got my attention and held me in bed for five hours.

No, what riveted me was the cosmic scope of the story. Shawnee had painted a picture with words, a picture of the world as it is. In concise, poetic language she had revealed to me the conflict, as she called it, "between the sunshine and the shadow." The shadow wasn't just suffering. It was evil; the wrongs man had perpetrated on himself for centuries and would likely continue to excoriate himself with for centuries more.

And yet, in spite of this weakness, this inherent flaw, Shawnee proved through her heroes that man could reach exquisite heights of virtue and beauty. That he was more than an animal or a random accident. He was a masterpiece in every sense of the word. And when he chose goodness, beauty, and truth above himself, he became even more magnificent.

Nothing I had read up to then had made this impression on me. Shawnee's book touched a chord in my soul that had lain dormant my entire life. Sitting in bed, staring at the wall, I realized I no longer wanted to cry. I was going to miss Shawnee a great deal when she died, and when it was time to say good-bye I *would* cry.

Looking down at the book in my hands, however, I understood a part of her would always be with me as long as I had her books. And a part of her would always be with her family and everyone else who had ever known her. Those who hadn't met her would be touched by her through these novels.

Stroking the cover of the book, I turned out the light and lay down to sleep, a glowing coal of comfort in my heart.

Over the next few months, Shawnee's health took a nose dive, just as she had expected. She sent me to Shane twice a week with a thumb drive and a journal or two, along with a letter detailing which books went with which series or where to find certain things on her thumb drive.

I met my future husband, John, on one of those trips. There was a hit-and-run I witnessed after visiting Shane, and John and I had to stabilize the man before the ambulance arrived to take him to the hospital. When I visited the accident victim in his hospital later on, I gave him a copy of one of Shawnee's books.

Through those last months, Shawnee's spirits remained high. She was as cheerful and sweet as a saint while her body deteriorated before our eyes. She became gaunt and hollow-eyed at last, as the doctors tried treatment after treatment to stall the cancer. I delivered her final batch of books a week before the fatal day came.

Shawnee's parents, Shane and his wife, and a few other family members were already there when I arrived. Half the nurses and doctors in the hospital were there, too. The other half had to remain on call, or they would have been there to see Shawnee one last time. A few were trying to stifle the sobs that they couldn't stop completely by pressing tissues to their noses. I had made sure to carry a nice, big box of tissues in my purse not long after my first run to see Shane, but I was determined not to cry all over Shawnee.

Victor was still in her lap when I arrived. Her breathing was shallow and raspy. But she smiled when she saw me. "Deirdre," she whispered.

"Hey, sweetie," I said, giving her a quick kiss on the forehead.

"What did you think of *Lantern and Sword*?"

"Beautiful," I said, a lump the size of a cantaloupe in my throat. But someone could have been strangling me and I would still have answered her. "The author really knows her stuff." I winked at her.

She smiled back. Raising a weak hand, she pointed to the model X-Wing on the table beside her bed. "Can you hang this up for me, please?"

I looked up at the ceiling, seeing for the billionth time the bare space above her head. "You betcha, honey."

As I picked up the model, I noticed a sticky note attached to the canopy. In Shawnee's graceful hand was written *For Deirdre*.

Biting back a sob, I stood on the stool Shane brought to me and hung the model above her bed. Shawnee looked up at it and smiled that familiar angelic smile. "All the lamps are lit," she murmured.

"They sure are, dear," her mother gasped. "They sure are."

Fifteen minutes later, she was gone. Cries went up throughout the room, but for some reason my eyes stayed dry. It was a lucky thing they did, or I would have missed what happened next along with most everyone else.

The minute Shawnee's breathing stopped, her toy Shield Liger shivered from head to tail. With the smooth grace of a living creature he stood up on her lap and shook himself. Then he took one step forward – and vanished into thin air.

I half wondered if I had blinked, he was gone so fast. But when I scanned the floor, I couldn't see him. It was as though a door had opened up in front of him and he had stepped straight through it.

Then something even more extraordinary happened. Moments after Victor disappeared, the room dimmed, as though a cloud passed in front of the window. I heard a sound like a collective sigh and, when the light came back, I had to swallow a yelp.

The many toys and posters that had adorned Shawnee's room were gone. The walls, which had not seen daylight for three years, were a sudden, blinding white. Dangling above Shawnee's bed, alone in an empty white sea, was the X-Wing she had left me.

Shane nudged my arm and pointed to the doorway as his wife went to comfort Shawnee's mother. I was just in time to see a red flash disappear around the corner. "She left them to the other kids in the hospital," he murmured. It took me a moment to realize that he was talking about the toys Shawnee had owned for the last three years. His voice was choked with tears. "All of them, except for your X-Wing and Victor. I guess they knew that before I did."

"Where did he go?" I whispered hoarsely.

"With her."

I looked back at Shawnee's still body, but she wasn't there anymore. The animating spirit had flown away at last; she was earthbound no longer. And where she had gone, Victor had been allowed to follow.

Distantly, I thought I heard a sound like a mighty roar. "Fly, Shawnee," I whispered, tears pricking my eyes. "*Fly!*"

All of this happened eight years ago, but I haven't forgotten a single detail of that day. No one but Shane and I saw Victor vanish from Shawnee's lap, and we were surprised when nobody else seemed to remember her toys and posters. It was as if they had somehow forgotten the marvelous den of myth and magic her room had been while she lived there. Even her parents didn't remember her room's décor while she was alive. They thought the only toy she had owned was the X-Wing she bequeathed me, and they were quite willing to let me have that.

Six months after Shawnee's death I married John. Two years later I quit nursing because I expected our first child. It was a few days after that when I read a column in the local paper trashing the latest novel Shane had released from her cache of stories.

Infuriated, I wrote a rebuttal that was published in the same paper, and my career as a writer was born. I haven't written much fiction yet, but the more children John and I have, the more I want to give them stories I know will help them grow up into good, responsible adults. They've all read Shawnee's published books, and the next one will, too.

Even now, Shane is still releasing her stories. Shawnee wrote eighteen novels and a plethora of short stories before she died, and that's not counting the previous ones from before we met. He says her thumb drives each contain a novel and a batch of stories, so he'll be publishing them for quite a while.

That's good, since he and his wife have another child on the way. Shawnee's twin younger brothers, who were born a year after she died, just like she said, they will need the money for college as well.

Shawnee was also right when she said the scientific community would go into apoplectic fits over her discoveries. But she was right, too, when she said it wouldn't matter. Thanks to Shane's friend in Congress, NASA built a ship based on one of her designs. It's been to the ISS thirty times and visited the moon on three different occasions. NASA's petitioned for more money to build some sister ships for it.

Shane told me they're also looking into her designs for a space station to replace the ISS and they've shown more than a little interest in her terraforming plan for Mars.

As for me, I keep writing. The model X-Wing Shawnee gave me is the only mobile our babies have ever had. And when John and I finally crawl into bed at night, I put one of her books underneath my pillow.

Sometimes, after I've had a really bad day, or some kind of calamity has befallen someone I care about, Shawnee visits me in my dreams. I never see her, but I can hear her laughing and singing. Though I can't remember the exact words, I know we've had conversations in these dreams.

There's a sort of mechanical sound that accompanies her voice, too, a kind of rhythmic pounding. It's like the sound of some giant running by me, and it always keeps time with her singing or her voice. The dreams never end without an animal roar accompanying the highest point of intensity in the song.

When I wake up from these dreams, I'm smiling and crying. John's usually awake before I am. He'll look at me, hand me the box of tissues he keeps on his bedside table, and says, "Was Shawnee by last night?"

"She was by," I answer him, before blowing my nose and sitting up. "And she told me 'All the lamps are lit'."

It took me a long time to figure out that Shawnee's last words were an admonition to all of us who loved her. "All the lamps are lit" was her way of telling us to keep living, to do what we were sent here to Earth to do. And her dream visits remind me that even when we die, our lights don't actually go out. They just move to a place where they're no longer earthbound.

A place where they're free…where they can finally *fly*.

GRANT SKELTON

Grant Skelton is a writer and author who lives near the buckle of the Bible Belt. He enjoys black coffee, black humor, and Black Sabbath. When not writing fiction, Grant contributes to New Noise Magazine (newnoisemagazine.com) and No Clean Singing (nocleansinging.com).

ATTRITION

By GRANT SKELTON

I used to hate my life. Hated waking up; hated going to sleep. Even hated sitting on my couch not doing jack shit. Now, I don't know. Like anything else, hating my life just uses up too much goddamn energy. Most of the time, I can't even muster up enough strength to indulge in some real quality suicidal ideation. That shit takes some intense concentration.

At first, I thought maybe I'd drink myself to death. And I tried it two or three times. But like anything else in life, reality didn't meet expectation. I envisioned falling asleep, bleary-eyed and swimmy-headed. Pictured myself floating in a tranquil ocean of spicy amber-colored whiskey. The sweet aroma of the aged oak barrel honey flooding my lungs until they ruptured. A relaxing death. So I thought. Drinking yourself to death isn't easy. Like I said, I tried it two or three times. And each time, all I managed to do was wake up with a jack-hammering headache. Plastering the seat of my pants to my ass was a layer of cakey, wooden petrified shit. Christ, how I vomited. I must've vomited up shit I ate when I was a fucking toddler. Vomited Creation itself. So yeah. Drinking yourself to death isn't as easy as it sounds.

If you count the two or three times I tried drinking myself to death, I guess you could say I've tried to kill myself two or three times. But thus far, I am unsuccessful. So that means I suck at it. I'm such a fuckup that I cannot even end my goddamn life correctly. Well, shit. I guess that means I'm consistent. If you're going to be a fuckup, at least make sure you fuck up consistently.

Aside from drinking myself into oblivion, my only other hobby is passively yearning for death. Now, I know what you're thinking. What in the name of fuck is a "passive" yearning? See, it's like this: I used to *actively* yearn for death. Hungered for it. Fucking *craved* the idea of leaving this fractured, pestilential blue orb and drifting off into the nebulous who-the-hell-cares beyond. Purgatory. Nirvana. Shit, Pee Wee's Cosmic Astral Fucking Playhouse. I don't fucking know. Something besides this. *Anything* has to be better than this! I'd even take being sodomized with a goddamn pitchfork for all eternity over this wasted, insipid existence. But, I digress.

I still want to die. But the more time passes, the more I find the intensity of that desire has waned. I don't know why. It isn't because I want to live. Let's not be ridiculous. If you have to choose between being bludgeoned once with a sledgehammer or bludgeoned a thousand times with a fucking tee-ball bat, I'm sure you'll pick the tee-ball bat. It doesn't mean you *want* to be bludgeoned with it. It just means that out of two shitty options, you picked the apparently-slightly-less-shitty of the two. So, that's what I mean by "passively" yearning for death. I still want to die, but I'm just not feeling the fire for it I used to. Not sure what happened. I guess like everything else in life, the zeal for it slowly drained out. So that's my life now. Sure as shit don't have any zeal for living. And, I'm getting close to empty on zeal for dying. Zeal is a slippery motherfucker.

I guess I do have one other hobby; hating my job. Cliché, right? I can hear you now. *No shit! Everyone hates their job! Take a goddamn number!* But it's beyond that. I didn't hate my life before I had this job. Sure, there were spurts here and there. Mostly in my adolescence, but that's another story. I didn't have to take medication for anxiety before

I had this job. Or depression. I take medication for that too. Slept pretty decent. Now, my doctor calls in a prescription every thirty fucking days just so I can get some goddamn inkling of what could be called *sleep*. Didn't used to drink this much either. Now, I stop drinking when I run out of alcohol, or I pass out. I've spent incalculable amounts of fucking money on mental health care. Copays for doctor visits. Copays for specialist visits. Copays for my goddamn shrink. Copays for medication. Copays for group therapy. The sons of bitches at my insurance company probably look at my file every day and go, *Holy shit! We're gonna see this crazy asshole on the news with a double-digit body count!* Trigger warning! Yep, I'm warning you I'm about to pull the fucking trigger!

Therapy. Now there's something worthwhile! My employee assistance program referred me to therapy. Outpatient, though. Unfortunately. If I had my way, I'd voluntarily commit myself. For life. I'd give a kidney for someone to tell me I was such a hazard to society that I had to be *put* somewhere. I'd take the straight jacket; settle for goopy applesauce and Nurse Ratched. Sure! Strap me down, tie me up, load me up with laudanum or morphine. Some shit that'll make me think I've died and gone to an afterlife that looks like it was designed by a kindergartener! Existence as I know it manifests in only eight colors. And none of them is inside the line. Purple snowmen. Blue rabbits. A sun with a smiley-face. Now that's a fucking afterlife!

So yeah, the employee assistance program referred me to therapy. Six weeks of it. I took it. Happily. It was six weeks I didn't have to be at my fucking job. And, I had the sick time saved up. So I got paid to go to therapy. I guess that's a fair trade. Least those assholes could do after making me hate my life.

The real bitch of all this is I don't have a *bad* life. My parents made their share of mistakes, but they never fucking abused me. I wasn't molested. Or beaten. Guess I might've gotten off on the wrong foot, but I don't have some God-awful, terrible, tragic fucking life. It's got its ups and downs. A couple of stories might make you cry. But all-in-all I've had a really good life. Before I hated my life, I loved it. Then I hated it. Then I hated the fact I hated it. And honestly, wish I still *hated* it. At least with hate there's passion. Not that it's good to hate your life. But at this point, I'd take hatred over apathy. Loathing of any sort, even self-loathing, is more utilitarian than apathy.

As an alternative to ending my life, I went back to school. Didn't finish my degree back in the day. Because, you know. Life and shit. One more thing I started and didn't finish. I went back to school. Conventional wisdom says, "You go back to school, you get your degree, you get a better job." Level the playing field. Qualify yourself. Goddamn conventional wisdom. I got the degree, paying for my tuition with overtime and income tax refunds. So now, I've qualified myself. I've leveled the playing field. And now I might as well stick my head into a goddamn industrial band saw. Same result as the degree. And a hell of a lot more interesting.

I've applied for other jobs coming up on two years. The best part? The silence. Not a rejection. Not a thanks, but we'll pass. Not even a fuck you. Just silence. Apply. Week goes by. Then a month. Send another email. Another month. Seriously, I'd rather someone came to my house and hit me in the dick with a fucking pickaxe than to just ignore me! At times, I've thought about rolling up into some of the places I've applied with a shotgun. Just with one shell, mind you. What do you think I am?! Some kind of homicidal lunatic? Shit, no. Just one shell. I'd march right into the hiring manager's office, throw my resume on his desk, put the shotgun in my mouth, and blow my goddamn head off. Where do I picture myself in 5 years? Haunting your dreams, you fucking asshole.

Two. Fucking. Years. I finally managed to land an interview. And that's where I've been since our conversation began. Yep, I've been ranting to you from the waiting room. To tell the truth, I don't even remember what they do here. Can't recall the name of the company either. Guess that doesn't exactly make me a great candidate does it? Fuck it. I got the interview. I should probably give more of a shit about my future. Well...shit.

The secretary (Executive assistant? Consumer relations supervisor? The bitch who answers the goddamn phone and shuffles papers all day. Her.) calls my name.

"Eldritch? Porter Eldritch?"

I stand up, buttoning my suit jacket, walk over to her desk, and rest my hands on the counter.

"Yes ma'am," I say. "I'm Porter Eldritch."

"The hiring manager is ready for you," the secretary says. "Follow me, please."

I comply. Fuck else I got to do, right? Went to the trouble of buying a suit. Worked double shifts for almost a month to be able to afford this goddamn thing. A notice a wrinkle in the sleeve of my jacket screams. All that, and still a wrinkle. Goddamn you, life. You're a sadist.

She prisses down the hall, like she's been doing it since grade school. You remember? The kinda kids who would show up early to clap erasers and wash the chalkboards? In between snorting lines of pencil shavings? Yep. Those kids. A bit ironic. Somehow I can't shake the feeling I'm in trouble and I'm going to the principal's office.

My shoes hew the skin from the insides of my feet. Pretty sure they'll be into the marrow by lunch.

The secretary stops in front of an open door. I peek inside and see windows. Not just *any* windows, mind you. Floor-to-ceiling windows. Outside, the city. The urban sprawl. Decaying tourist traps splattered with the visage of our rock n' roll messiah. Bricks, mortar, concrete, asphalt. Things that used to be dreams in somebody's mind. Now husks prostrating themselves beneath this window.

I go in and turn to the right. I see a desk, no wait. That's not entirely accurate. It's wide enough to fit maybe forty people. And a few friends. And it's so neat and sparsely decorated with two or three of the latest Apple tablets. Jesus. This isn't a desk. It's a goddamn *altar.* Somewhere Steve Jobs is looking down with favor and blessing upon the house of his faithful acolyte.

Sitting behind said altar - er, desk is a man with impeccable side-parted hair. A suit infinitely better looking than the hand-me-down rag I hung on myself (albeit fewer wrinkles). He's got a five o'clock shadow. Which isn't a problem, by any means. But he's got that kind of intentional five o'clock shadow. The sort that shave it just enough to let you know they're old enough to grow facial hair. And his smile. I wish

I could say it was a smirk. But it's not. It's a genuine fucking article. His name's probably Hampton or Alec or Seamus or something.

On the wall over his head I see three diplomas. Bachelor's in information technology. Bachelor's in computer science. Master's in business management. I should smash those glass frames right now. Open my wrists all over the fucking diplomas just to see his authentic business management smile fade off his goddamn face.

"Mr. Eldritch!" he says, putting out his hand.

I reach out and take it. We shake. What do you think I am? Some kind of asshole?

"Good to meet you," he says. "My name is Tristan Vogue. Friends call me TV!"

Well, shit. Could be worse. His initials could be "VD."

"Nice to meet you, Tristan —"

He cuts me off. He's totally fucking serious.

"Please," he says, "TV."

Ok. Your life, shitheel. "Good to meet you, T...V..."

"Something to drink?" TV asks.

"Coffee?"

"A cappuccino then? Maybe a latte? Whipped cream?"

"Ah," I mutter. "Black?" Hadn't meant that to be a question.

"Black?" he says, looking like I just tossed a giant turd on his shoes.

"Yeah." Black as the swirling corpse of the collapsed star that used to be my future. Jesus. Wish I'd have seen that coming at my high school career fair.

"Very well," TV huffs. "You know, my granddad used to drink his black. Always with a cigarette. Do you smoke?"

"Nah," I say. "Quit yesterday."

"And how's that going for you?"

"I quit today, too. And tomorrow again, more than likely."

"What a wit!" TV laughs. "Are you always so dry and honest?"

"Long as I've got a pulse."

"Ha! Please," he says. "Do have a seat."

"Thanks."

He steps to a table in the corner of his office. I hear the magic sound of the caffeinated elixir being poured into a cup. TV hands it to me. Inside the cup is a tiny city. Our city. Same godforsaken concrete cesspool as the painstaking panorama out the window. I shift the cup in my hands, watching the steaming black liquid wash over the tiny city. Little bankers, real estate agents, digital content assholes and IT motherfuckers all being ripped in half. Pulled away from their tablets and bicycles and four-day weekends. Their statuesque skin boiling off in the festering, noxious rancor of their own shit. Shit and self-indulgence.

"Mr. Eldritch? Sir?"

"Huh?"

"Something wrong with your drink?"

The little city is gone. I sip.

"Nothing's wrong," I lie. "Just admiring the aroma. It's very...potent."

"It is good, isn't it? Get it fresh from Whole Foods every month."

"Yeah."

"So," TV says. "You applied on our online job board for the...digital security supervisor position."

"Sure did."

"And how did you hear about us?"

"Google," I answer.

"And if I used the phrase 'search engine optimization,' would you know to what I was referring?"

I swig down the last of my coffee. "Your page is first," I say.

"Excellent!" TV says. "Now tell me a little bit about your work history. What do you think qualifies you for the digital security supervisor position?"

The dogs. First thing that came to my mind. One German shepherd. Female. One Jack Russell. Male. Last winter, we got a right proper ice storm. Power was out for over a week. Utility poles falling down all across the city. Life came to a rapid halt. We just aren't prepared for shit like that here. Ol' Jack Frost caught us with our pants down and shoved his long round icicle right up our chimney. The dogs. Asshole left them outside. All. Fucking. Night. Still alive when we first got there. Thick layer of hard ice covering their bodies. They'd been frozen to the ground. Did you know that dogs can cry? Just like people. Only, they're better at it.

"Well, I've done security for a whole community for years now. And we use technology to help out with reporting. And data." Then the train crash. You don't know how many tiny parts are in an automobile until you've seen what happens when it goes up against a train. It folds over and over itself like a fucking aluminum can. So thin and brittle. The Mom was driving. Texting on her phone. Went around the railroad crossing arm. Guess she didn't hear the bell. Train was already on the tracks. The two little ones in the back weren't buckled into their car seats right. After the impact, their bodies. Well, they weren't bodies anymore. They'd been compressed and mashed into the crinkled metal of the car. Metal, plastic, rubber. And some soft, tender, pieces of. Shit, it looked like fruit. All ground up and blended together. Teddy bear and a Barbie were the only things in one piece.

"I've dealt with chaotic incidents. And dangerous people."

Simone Jones. Eleven–years-old. She was asleep in her bedroom. Just finished writing a book report, her Mom told me that night. In her bed in Thor pajamas. Her favorite superhero, her Mom said. She was going to be Thor for Halloween. But she didn't get to. The first round penetrated the outside of the house, through the living room, into Simone's bedroom. It ended up in her left hip, shattering her pelvis. The second round went right through the stomach of the thunder god himself, and subsequently into Simone's stomach. The last one penetrated her left cheek and came out the other side of her skull. We found seventeen rifle casings outside the house. Never found out what an eleven-year-old girl could've done to deserve getting shot at with that kind of ammunition. Guess she just picked the wrong night to sleep in her own bed. Goddamn you, life. You evil motherfucker.

"I see your resume says you're a police officer," TV says. "Why is it that you want to leave the department to come work here?"

I could tell him it's to save my marriage. To spare my family becoming a suicide statistic. Cops' divorce rate is about twice the national average, give or take. Suicide rate's about that as well. I'm in my second month of therapy for substance abuse. So I could say something like, "I'm actively seeking wellness of my mind by looking for something with a better work-life balance." I guess all that's true. But I need to play the part of a progressive, well-adjusted entrepreneurial type who's got his ducks in a row. Or at least got them on the same fucking planet.

"I'm looking for a challenge," I lie. "I'm trying to see the full manifestation of my potential. I want to transcend past my weaknesses, actualize my emotional quotient, and partner with a unique group of people with a common mission and a shared goal."

I think I read that on some life coach's blog. See, life? You're not the only sardonic bastard around here.

"Wonderful!" TV says. "I've got to tell you, Mr. Eldritch, when your resume first came across my desk my curiosity radar instantly went up."

"Thanks."

"Absolutely. I know a go-getter when I see one," TV says. "And you're definitely a go-getter."

"'Preciate that."

TV stands up from his desk. He rests his palms on it, looking down his nose at me. Teeth look like they're made out of marble. And his eyes. So sparkly they look like props.

"But unfortunately, I think you'd be better suited to continue in your current career path."

"Come again?"

"You're clearly great doing what you're doing now! Why would you want to change something great for something ordinary?"

Why would I want a change? Can't think of a reason. My drinking habit, maybe? DTs from when I go too long without drinking. The seven different kinds of medication I have to take, and then all the other shit I take to counteract the side effects. Does pressing your duty weapon to your temple during your shift count as an actual suicide attempt? Or do you actually have to pull the trigger? What if the round is a dud? Is it still an "attempt?"

Ordinary. I'd donate my fucking hypothalamus for an "ordinary" day. A day without overdose deaths, parents whipping their kids with extension cords, prostitutes getting sodomized with beer cans, people shooting each other over social media threats. Goddamn, I've seen a lot of people die. *That's my ordinary.* Give me a schmuck asshole boss ten years my junior who's pissed that I missed the meeting. If that was my biggest problem, I wouldn't be happy. But I might be less miserable, if only by a margin.

I stand up and walk over to TV's desk, smile my biggest shit-eating grin and snatch up his stapler. I grab his shoulder and force the stapler into his custom-tailored pie hole. I squeeze the stapler down on the moist pinkness of his tongue. I pull. Slowly at first, then harder. And harder. TV squeals. His eyes flood with tears. He groans incomprehensibly. And that's when he hears it. The wet, plopping squelch of his tongue slowly separating from the back of his throat. Steamy gouts of blood jet out from his mouth. They slather down his shirt, cascading over his pants and onto the floor. I twist the stapler over. TV's purple face quivers, his feeble cries reverberate off the grandiose windows. I shift my weight back, setting TV's tongue loose from his bleeding, ulcerated throat. His tongue, a raw loin on a butcher's hook, hangs from the stapler. He falls forward with a heave and a tremor. I drop the sopping stapler next to his face.

"How's that for ordinary you fucking scumbag?" I ask.

A foam of bubbly blood gurgles from his mouth.

"Piece o' shit," I say, making my way to the door.

"Thanks for coming in."

I turn around. TV's standing behind his desk? His thumbs in his pockets. His mouth is intact, and the stapler secure on his desk. His clothes are just as tidy as when I first arrived.

"Sorry to have wasted your time," he says.

"No," I say. "It's me who's sorry. Sorrier than you'll ever know."

I open the door and leave.

That night at work, I answered a few calls. Loose dog. Couple of verbal domestic arguments. An auto theft at a gas station where the driver left the car running at the pump. Went inside to pay for gas. Came back outside. Poof. Car's gone. It gets cold in the winter, I get it. We all like to be warm. Some people like it enough to take it from somebody else.

Once the calls for service began to die down, I drove my squad car onto a disheveled dead-end street with so many potholes it looked like a goddamn cheese grater. A little hiding place we sometimes drive to in order to finish up reports. Eat, when possible. Fortunately for me there's nobody from my shift back here. Not at the moment, anyhow. This is where I've planned to do it. To end my life. And tonight's the night.

I unzip my uniform shirt and hang it on a wire coat hanger. I hang the coat hanger from the "oh shit" handle above the front passenger's side door, unstrap my bullet proof vest and lean it against the driver's seat. I unbuckle my duty belt clasps, remove my belt, roll it up, and drop it onto the driver's seat. Squeezing the grip of my Sig Sauer P229, I defeat both of the safeties on the holster and draw the weapon. Something in me doesn't want to get my uniform bloody.

There's a three-by-five photo of my wife and my two boys in my wallet. My wife, Madison is in the middle in an orange sundress with patterns of dark red leaves. She said it made her miss the autumn. Leaning in to her left is my older son. Quinton. He's four. Hair so curly you couldn't straighten it with an iron. He's smiling a big, toothy grin. But his eyes always look like he's about to cry. In Madison's right arm is Nathaniel, our infant. Two bright, round cheeks that look like scoops of ice cream. He's extremely ticklish, most so on his neck.

Eleven years Madison and I have been married. 4,098 days, to be exact. I work third shift though. So I guess technically it's 4,099.

Can't tell you exactly why I want to die. Could be the anxiety and depression that went untreated for almost thirty years. Could be my drinking. Horrible diet, bad sleeping. I had a good childhood. Got along great with Mom and Dad. My bills are paid. No outstanding debts. No car payments. Madison and I planned to pay off our mortgage early. Could've been done in 2 years.

Could be the job. You get into this line of work because you want to help people. Protect the innocent. Help the needy, the kids, the elderly. The vulnerable. But I'm the vulnerable one. This city, it eats people. Strong, weak, old, young. It doesn't discriminate. All flesh is equally appetizing. People call it a community. And it's got houses. And fences. And parks. Real estate. But we're cannibals, all of us. And me most of all. I *need* to feel other people's despair. To consume it. So when I look into the future with Madison, Quinton, and Nathaniel, I see my body. My face smiling. It resembles me. But the real me, the inner me. My psyche, my soul...my shit, essence, I guess. It isn't there. It's been eaten. By the city. By this job. I am not there. So if I can't be there, I may as well not be there.

I stuff the photo into my cargo pocket. Tilting my head back, I insert the barrel of my duty weapon into my mouth. The cold steel barrel scrapes my uvula and I gag. Jesus. I'm trying to *use* the fucking thing. Not *eat* it. I move the barrel forward onto my tongue. Yes. This is the way. No. No, wait. I could break my jaw. Shatter my teeth. Well, shit. Somebody's going to find me! I can't have someone finding my body when I look like a toothless asshole with a broken jaw! So I move the pistol beneath my chin. This is better...isn't it? What if I miss my brain? What if the bullet doesn't penetrate my skull and just goes around it? And I end up with some fucked up patchwork scar and my hair won't grow back? That can happen.

Maybe I should try from the side. I press the barrel to my right temple. Yeah. This is right. The pressure against my head is oddly calming. Like my brain sees through the barrel into a long, dark, steel tunnel. On the other side of the tunnel is relief. Release. Emancipation. I don't want there to be an afterlife. I'm not looking for heaven. I want to be nowhere. Or rather, I don't want to be. I just want to iris out. You know, how old TV shows used to do? The black borders of the screen slowly close in, forming a small circle in the middle. And then the circle gets smaller and smaller, a black quilt of peaceful nothingness encroaching upon the screen. Iris out. That's what I want on the other side. A warm, calm, soothing, sheet sweeping over me. Lulling me into a slumber of nonexistence.

"F82," the dispatcher's voice comes over the radio. "F82, did you read the call?"

Within a breath, I'm on my feet scurrying back to my car. I yank open the door, trip and fall. My face very nearly collides with the console radio. I pick up the mic, hold the button, and speak.

"F82, I'm sorry. I missed the call. Please repeat."

"F82, check for a noise complaint in the 1300 block of Nolan St.

near the intersection of Nolan St and Kendrick Blvd. Complainant refused. Advised of loud hammering. F82."

"F82, check," I reply. "Coming from 677 Cropsey."

It's then when I realize I still had my pistol in my other hand. Don't even remember putting it in my other hand. Fine motor skills, indeed. Duty calls. Goddamn you, life. Sick sense of humor you've got.

I throw my vest and shirt on, strap my duty belt around my waist. In such a hurry, I probably look like a foot-long hotdog crammed into a half-foot bun. What the hell though, right? Only a noise complaint.

I make my way through the streets. Night. Only time the city is beautiful. Sure, even the potholes have potholes. Dilapidated shotgun shacks with collapsing roofs. Gutted, rusted cars parked in grass three feet high. Old edifices of mortar and brick that used to be barber shops or grocery stores. Windows smashed, doors kicked in, graffiti over peeling paint. But at night, that stuff's harder to see. Night makes the ruin attractive. Call it blight if you want. If the apocalypse ever does come, this is what the world will be like. The silence takes my breath away. Go out into the country for some solitude if you like. Out here, at this time of day, you won't hear so much as a cricket. And one day, the crickets might be here will be gone too. Part of me wishes I could live to see that. The quiet of a city cleansed of its most cancerous infection – us. What repose that kind of quiet could bring!

When I make it to Nolan and Kendrick, I pick up the mic.

"F82 in the area," I say.

"F82, area," responds dispatch. "Advise if additional units are needed."

"F82, check."

Dispatch said the complainant heard noises coming from this area. Funny. We never get calls on this street. The last person to live here was Ms. Kimona Oleander. She was a school teacher at one time. Taught for nearly thirty years. Somewhere around year twenty, she got into crack cocaine. Pair that with a drinking habit and you've got a career killer. Even so, she lived to the ripe old age of eighty-eight. Lived at 1401 Nolan. The dead end of the street. Railroad tracks on the other side, but no trains ran on them the whole time I've worked here. Anyhow, Ms. Oleander died three years ago now. Or was it four?

"F82," I say into my mic. "Could you call the complainant back and see if they can provide a more specific location?"

"Negative, F82," dispatch answers. "Complainant called from a disconnected cell phone."

Of-fucking-course.

"Check," I say.

I park my car, shut off the ignition, and get out. Streetlights have been out on this street since forever. If the city even put any bulbs in the motherfuckers, that is. I dig my flashlight out of its pouch and turn it on. I pull my pistol and hold it behind my right thigh with the barrel pointing down. Always be prepared, yeah?

"Hello?" I call out. "Police officer. Anyone out here?"

Several mechanical thuds. Sounds like someone hammering a nail that doesn't want to cooperate. Seems to be coming from 1324 Nolan. Surprised this house actually has visible numbers on it. The mailbox is tilted at an awkward angle toward the street, its door hanging open. The rusty metal screws groan in the late autumn breeze. Makes the thing sound like it's laughing at me.

The roof of 1324 Nolan sags in the middle. Tree must've fallen on it at some point. Jagged cracks crisscross over the concrete driveway, like some cosmic spiral-shaped mouth that's about to open up and swallow me. That'd be on Sports Center's highlight reel next week for certain.

I meander across the walkway toward the front door. Then the hammering again. *Bang. Bang. Bang. Bang.*

"Shit!" I yell.

"F82. Start another car to 1324 Nolan. Think I've got somebody inside. Possibly armed with a hammer."

Dispatch acknowledges.

From where I stand, I can see the front door dangling from the single top hinge. Its gentle sway hypnotizes me for a moment.

"Guh," comes a plea from inside the house. "Help!"

"Fuck," I whisper. "Here we go."

I run toward the front door and shove it open. With my duty weapon at my hip, I peer around both sides of the threshold. From my vantage point, I can't see anyone.

"Police! Drop the weapon and step out where I can see you."

"Help!"

This one sounds more like a wet, gurgling plop than a human voice. Like someone dropping a freshly soaked mop onto a linoleum floor. I ease myself across the threshold, trying to cover myself from all angles.

"F82," I whisper into the radio. "Might have a victim inside. I'm entering the house. Have additional units expedite."

Dispatch orders more cars to respond.

The luminous cone of my light darts across a decomposing floor. Cockroaches skitter over the walls. A grotesque, hairy rat bounds across the hallway.

"Jesus, fuck!" I curse.

"Hhhhhelp," someone cries.

I run toward the sound, nearly tripping over my own feet in the darkness. In the living room, or what I presume used to be a living room, someone is leaning against the wall. Looks like a man. He's facing me. His body twitches rhythmically, leaning at the hip to the right while jerking the left shoulder.

"Police!" I yell. "Drop your weapon. I will shoot!"

"Helllppp mmmeee…"

I cautiously make my way over to where he is standing. Both of his arms hang at his sides, blood on his face. I holster my pistol, just about to check his pulse when I see his face. He doesn't have one. Not anymore. The skin of his forehead, his nose, and cheeks has been peeled back. Like someone would do with an orange rind. Underneath is exposed subcutaneous leathery strips of muscle. And beneath that, the porcelain shine of his skull. The skin around his mouth seems just intact enough for him to utter only the most rudimentary of syllables. His eyes wobble from their sockets like ripe cherries.

Jutting out from his chest is a long, smooth spike. Blotched with speckles of yellow, green, and brown. And it's impaled him to the wall.

"Hhhhelllppp…" he croaks.

I drop my flashlight and wrap my hands around the spike. Heaving all my weight against it, I try to pull it out. The spike emits an eardrum-puncturing shriek that makes my head swim. Small, thorny tendrils reach up from its surface. They gauge through my hands and wrap themselves around the bones of my fingers. Like barb-wire tentacles, they burrow into my bones and throb against the inside. They retract with such force, my bones snap like pencils, shredding my hands into pieces. Below my wrists, thin ribbons of bloody minced flesh and splintered bone have taken the place of my hands.

Deafened by my own screams, I don't hear it until it's right behind me. The hammering first. Something shoots through my chest and hurls me against the wall. Gasping, I look down and see another spike. Just like the one in the man on the wall next to me. Inside my chest, the spike expands its thorny digits into my lungs and heart. Like ten thousand snakes all slithering into my chest at the same time. Sinking their fangs into me in unison. I vomit a thick gout of viscous, mucky black bile. Most of which just sticks to the inside of my mouth.

It walks like a person. It has two lower appendages you could call feet. They look more like purple and black mushroom stalks. The skin is translucent, sparks of blue and yellow light visibly worming their way through its body. It gives off a smell so fetid the bile in my throat is something of a relief. It has four gaunt, withered arms protruding from its gelatinous torso. In the center of the torso is a crooked, oval-shaped orifice. Inside this massive, abyssal maw are several pasty, pulsating, conical tongues. Each one ejaculates an issue of frothy, sweltering pus. Just above the mouth, a single, luminescent green eye. From the ghastly gangrene eyelids grow sharp, pointed branches that appear to function as lashes.

One of the withered hands reaches into the eye and takes hold of a lash. The lash frees itself from the eyelid with a sound not unlike a fish-hook pulled from an unsuspecting thumb. The creature lets out a throaty roar and hurls the lash at me. It pierces through my stomach, the tendrils razing through my intestines down into my bowels.

The creature lumbers toward me, its translucent skin blubbering over its feet like water in an enema bag. I focus on the sparks of light zooming about inside the creature's body. They begin to synchronize, dancing together like a family of alien fireflies. The four tubal tongues bob as the mouth inches toward my face.

In the lights of the creature's skin; it's the city. Not the buildings or the pavement or the politicians or the musical heritage. But what's under all of that. The scum under the drain. The dust under the bed. It's the history of the city from before my time. Before my grandfather's time. It's plantations and floggings and men owning other men. It's revolt and civil disobedience and reprisals and unrest. All manner of brutality and corruption. The fear and hatred we have for our neighbors. The disgust of dehumanizing otherness along the lines of class, race, national origin. This is the city I swore to protect. The city that eats its own young before they open their eyes. This is my city.

Unable to move, unable to break my gaze away from the floating lights. It's then I have my last conscious thought. In spite of my paralysis, the corners of my mouth fidget into a manic smile. I'm going to be chewed, swallowed, and digested. And then I will, very literally, be shit.

Goddamn you, life. You fucking asshole.

ROB ROWNTREE

Rob Rowntree lives in Notting-hamshire, England, with his wife and two boys. He took up writing fiction over ten years ago and has had some success with short stories, notably, Armadillo, in issue two of the short-lived professional magazine, Farthing. More recently his work has appeared in the 27 Stories from Owl Canyon Press, 2019, Transtories Anthology, from Aeon Press and the anthology Colinthology (in memory of the SF writer Colin Harvey), from Wizards Tower Press. Unbound Brother's is his first novel. He is currently working on his second, Slow Sky.

CHOKE

BY ROB ROWNTREE

'Seductive sky,
Harbinger of death clothed in sunrises loved, and
Sunsets wrought from heavenly pastel sprays, and yet
A dust came calling, crawling down that russet sky,
Bleeding.'

Fingers, just so:

In the market place the punishments continued.

Six bowed heads, six out-stretched arms, hands splayed and teth-ered, six lopped off thumbs. Food was scarce, a problem; stealing it a bigger problem. Daavid watched for a while; then, his civic duty fulfilled, he reached up, adjusted his filter mask, turned, and walked away. Victims came in many flavours these days.

The town ranged across the landscape in a rough circle about the wide-open market place. Under the dour, dust filled sky it hugged the rolling hills like a shanty blanket, each patch a quilted hovel. Ahead, dust rolled in drifts, higher where it settled against buildings, broken carts, and tipped rubbish.

Daavid angled his face skyward, squinting against the constant fine grit. The interstellar particulates filled the grey sky; darker shadows drifted and swirled in corrupted wind patterns. Blinking, he looked to the sun, its historically cloud-shaded pale orb now riven with visible black lines as the stellar cloud showered down its load on star and planet alike; victims both to the universe's whim.

Sensing a slight build up on his cheek, Daavid shook his head to remove the dust from his dark skin, turned up his coat collar against a pervasive chill and further irritation before trudging on.

In the distance, light flooded the gloom. Through the falling motes, the town's generating station poured a torpid glow from windows, doorways and cracks. Even here, two kilometres away, Daavid heard the high-pitched hum of hundreds of stationary bicycles. A marvel really, born of need and a little human ingenuity. Each resident took a two-hour slot, pedalling furiously to hold back the night. Futile? Possibly, but it gave people hope.

He knew of a couple of oil burners operating down the coast, and rumours circulated of an old nuclear plant still running over on the other side of the country. But there'd been no news recently. No news for years.

Like a gentle thief, the dust snuck in, measured the task ahead, and set in for the long haul. There'd been soothing commentary at the time. 'The interstellar dust would burn up in the atmosphere... get distributed by the wind... wouldn't be in amounts to bother us'.

Slowly it came, built, and before long aeroplanes stopped flying, ships started sinking, and transport infrastructures collapsed. Then - anarchy.

But seven years in and this small community, to some extent, bucked the trend. The light ahead reassured, at once testament to people's tenacity and a remembrance of better times. A comfort.

Daavid smiled a little. Pride perhaps, but also the knowledge his current pedalling stint lay days away, made his mood a little lighter.

Striding through the mounting dust, he skirted a clearance team ploughing the streets clean, and nipped into an empty rice bar. He'd grab a sesame rice cake (god bless the illuminated hydro-barns), before moving on. Fuel for the day; from the sound of his work-brief, there'd be no time later. Being *consultant* to the town's law enforcement had its perks, but lunchbreaks weren't one of them.

Four bodies they said: laid out in the power-plant's court yard. Each a stranger, each lying face-up to the sky.

Disgruntled employees? Why would they kill strangers?

The rice cake tasted dry, nutty. The sky rained dirt and Daavid wondered about victims. Everyone was a victim in one way or another. Right?

Crowded with Constables, the courtyard reminded Daavid of the old food distribution points, police holding back over-eager customers.

A cordon boxed off the central space, and within Sheppard and Crow fussed over their crime scene employees.

"Sheppard."

The lean officer turned and absently brushed dust from her balding head. "Daavid. Always nice to see you."

"Yeah, right," Crow added

Daavid ignored the station banter, ducked under the cordon, and walked over to the bodies. Four as advised; laid out on their backs in a side-by-side row. Dust already obscured their clothing with a powdery centimetre or so of grey.

On first inspection, no obvious signs of foul play presented, no blood pooled, no torn or damaged clothing. True, the dust might hide evidence, but—

"So, you see anything? Got that special mojo working yet?" Sheppard appeared playful, not an unusual trait for her, but today it felt forced, almost a dare.

Daavid walked to the nearest body, crouched by the head, and reached out to gently brush the dust from the face. A woman, mid-thirties, blonde hair. Something held her mouth open.

He glanced quickly at the three remaining bodies and saw a

depression in the dust covering their mouths. Held open? Open to the sky? *Ritual?*

"Have your guys messed with this?"

"Right." Crow turned his back and stepped away. Daavid ignored the obvious dismission.

Sheppard said, "It's no end-of-d'world scam. Though I don't see how that would matter now."

Daavid sighed, stood, and approached Sheppard. "Fine, I just want to do my job, file the report, and go home and take a cold bath. Can we just get on without the sardonic shit?"

"Ain't shit. They tell us we'll be out of the cloud in five years. Looks like we might not last that long. Just expressing an opinion during my day-to-day. No harm intended."

Raising his hands palms outward, Daavid said, "Good. So, they've been left untouched by your crime scene guys."

"They ain't got to the heads yet."

"Well then, they missed their chance."

Daavid knelt, dug his hand deep into the dead woman's open mouth, his fingers brushed something cold and hard. Grasping hold, he pulled the object free. A small burp followed, releasing a scent of spice, dead meat.

Turning his hand over he saw a large brooch, pin extended. The broach held a frosted scattering of stars over a green dome. On the reverse a name, Fiona Tobin.

"Crow, check the other mouths and get your guys to brush the dust away; I want a good look at them."

Crow looked to Sheppard and Daavid appreciated the small nod given to her subordinate. It wasn't often he could enjoy his 'special' position within the local community, and each little win counted, at least to him.

Three more brooches, three more names.

Sheppard said, "It's ritualistic. Laid out just so, facing the sky. Meticulous."

Daavid thought it certainly looked that way, but it didn't feel right. Dust removed; no signs of violence were apparent. No clues to any potential cult, religion, or whacked out belief. Nothing, just four cold bodies eating brooches. "Too early to say, Sheppard. Do we have any witnesses? Night guard, workers, anything?"

"Nope. Not a one."

"Arrange for the bodies to be taken back to the station's ice-house. Maybe there are disfigurements to be found on their skin, but I doubt it." David raised his hand and waved the brooch about. "I'll go and check these out."

"You will?"

Sheppard appeared confused. Daavid said, "Do keep up."

Crow added, "Right."

Sheppard opened her mouth but before she could speak, Daavid smiled and added, "The observatory. They're all astronomers."

"Astronomers?" Sheppard waved a hand at the sky. "In this muck? Seems rather redundant."

"Someone's got to keep an eye on this stuff. Let us know when it's ending, when to prepare."

Sheppard barked a hoarse laugh, coughed. "They can't see shit. Old satellites are long gone. What can they measure?"

"That." Daavid pointed toward the pale, sick orb of the Sun. "They measure how much light is coming from that."

"S'all double talk and mumbo-jumbo. More dust, less dust, a gentle easing of atmospheric burden. Just words."

Just words.

Daavid glanced at the hollow, open mouths filling with dust, choking. *Was it that easy? Was it symbolic?*

"Okay Sheppard, I'll catch you later. And Crow, see if you can learn a few new phrases by tonight. Maybe we can have a full conversation."

Daavid, hardly heard the replied "right", as his mind raced. Ritual or murder?

Squeeze:

The observatory surmounted the crest of a low hill, a dome

surrounded by a flat circular building. Its dust quilted exterior gave it the countenance of an old ruin, a buried relic.

Light played in a few grimy windows. Open double-doors gave a cold invite to a shadowed interior. Looked wrong, abandoned.

Halting, Daavid allowed his training to kick in, hours and hours of repetitive drills held him still, shouted to get back-up, but how would he do that? Go back and fetch help, bring back a team? Was there any point? A weight shifted, pushed protocol aside, and Daavid moved on. He pulled a flashlight from his pocket, a perk, and allowed his tired mind to enjoy its heft, its status. Life felt squashed, why not break the rules a little, push past the expected.

Foolish, but what the hell. He could always justify his action with a need to rescue prospective victims. And again, the concept of a world full of victims rose to tug at his imagination. Of course, people had always waved the flag of victimisation to justify things. Smiling, Daavid wondered why he shouldn't use the same.

Glass crunched under his feet.

Brighter inside than he'd hoped, Daavid shone his flashlight into dark corners and darker doorways. Nothing. Reception lay deserted, chairs and desks littered the corridors, and a faint hum pervaded the air, like an electrical motor straining.

Removing his mask and breathing deeply, Daavid tasted a faint ionisation, dust; the ash like flavour unpleasant but familiar hid another sour note, blood.

Replacing his filter, he drew his sidearm, chose a direction, and walked on.

He needed to find someone, anyone, and he guessed the observatory dome might be a good a place as any to start.

Ten paces and a muffled voice from a side room could be heard. Hesitating, he placed his foot down gently, weight on the balls of his feet. Remaining motionless, he listened.

It came quiet, a whisper, no more, and he couldn't make out the words. A sob? No, more like a gasp. What? Straining, he realised he'd stumbled upon a couple of people.

He heard subdued tones, whispers of acquiescence and intimacy. Although distinct words eluded him, their tenor felt unmistakeable.

Silently he edged over to the wall and poked his head around the door-jamb. The sounds stopped.

Realising his basic error, he dodged out of the doorway, stood flat against the wall, thought better of it, and crouched down. The walls would be thin, bullets were fast, hard.

"Hey," he said.

Nothing. Were they scared? Or waiting for an opportunity to strike, or maybe escape?

"Listen. I don't know what's going on here. Much rather be home eating an old can of tuna. Over at the power-plant there are some bodies, colleagues of yours, the Constables asked me to check things out."

Nothing, then rustling, a sob.

"Name's Oduba. Daavid Oduba. You're frightened, I get it. I don't know why, but looking around here I can understand it."

Muffled voices. No reply.

"Fine. Let me talk then. Between this doorway and the entrance is clear. Nobody but me between you and the entrance. Guess you hid in there when whatever went down happened. If you want out, there's nothing to stop you." He felt awkward then. They'd been making love, why would they want out?

A small voice said, "You there?"

"Candida, don't engage him."

"Why not? Doesn't really matter anymore does it."

Daavid said, "Hi Candida, name's Daavid. I'm not going to hurry you. Take your time, your friend too."

After a few seconds a laugh came, a nervous, ironic giggle. "Time. You hear that Kam, time he says."

"Candida." Kam appeared cross.

Daavid edged away, opening up some space along the wall. "Listen, I don't know what's happened, and if it helps you, although it irks me not to ask questions, I'll move down the hall opening up a clear route for you to leave by. Just slip by and leave." Risky, he knew, but he'd always believed giving a little resulted in rewards. Hopefully, he'd get some answers.

"Mister. Daavid." Candida sounded tired, or–

"Candida, you taken any stims?" Daavid hated stim rages. Unpredictable, dangerous.

"What if I have? It hardly matters. I'll be accepting your offer." Addressing her friend, she added, "You coming?"

Daavid stood and said, "Right, I'm moving by the door, don't shoot me or nothing." He moved quickly, silently, offering them a brief shadowed target. Further down the hallway he stopped and crouched low.

The hallway held a dull illumination, grey light oozed in from the broken double-doors. A head bobbed out of the doorway and darted straight back. Then a more cautious glance.

"S'okay," Daavid offered.

Slowly, two silhouettes emerged. Holding hands, they hesitated before backing away toward the doors. One of them stopped. Candida? "We were making out, that's all. Anyone would, you know."

"Well yeah, I guess." Daavid hoped his confusion didn't show. Making out? In this mess. The destroyed furnishings and damaged walls spoke of mayhem, violence, madness. Just making out. "What happened?"

Candida's silhouette shrugged. "Sometimes there's no point to anything other than satisfying a desire or dream." Then, in what Daavid thought of as wistful tone, she added, "There's always tomorrow."

"Don't follow?"

"Mister, you should just leave, go home. There's nothing for you here. Nothing for anyone."

"Thanks for the advice."

Candida laughed, before they both turned and edged away.

Rising to his feet, Daavid stepped backward and immediately stumbled over an upturned table. Gazing up from the jumbled mess on the floor, staring at the scratched stained walls, and listening to a steady drip of far off water, Daavid wondered what in the heck he'd fallen into.

Carefully standing, he brushed at a damp patch on his coat. It splashed a row of dots across the worn and dusty fabric.

Further in, he came to the observatory dome. A sign above the door read, 'Solar Luminosity Observatory – Project Employees Only.' Daubed across the lettering in bright yellow paint someone had scrawled, 'Solar Necrosis'. Daavid shook his head and stepped over the threshold.

In the gloom, he saw a large diameter device angled up on a gimballed platform. Small pinpoint LEDs bled sharp reds and blues onto the floor. Power. And as he strained to hear, he detected a low hum, perhaps the gimballed mount still turned.

Above, an odd arrangement of baffles fed the ever-falling dust away from the telescope's open end and into large wheeled, high walled carts. They overflowed now, but Daavid guessed emptying them would keep the room and its equipment running smoothly.

Beyond the central area, a bank of monitors hissed and sparked. No images though.

Nothing here. The place felt as empty as the bodies back in the power plant. A dust covered mystery. Perhaps the Constables knew more now.

Deciding to head back, Daavid resolved to make sure he had all the available information before heading home. A clue lay somewhere within the facts; a little thought, a drink, some food, and who knew… cases had been solved on less.

The streets hustled with thronging people, heads bent, masks pulled tight, and eyes cast down. Workers heading home to the illusory safety of the indoors. Shut the world out, shut the grit-swollen night away. What had Candida said, 'there's always tomorrow'.

He angled against the flow of streaming people, shoved by and pushed through. No exclamations greeted his aggressive parting of the ways, no derogatory comments, but rather an acceptance of the way things were, the way the world was now.

The station came into view. A rusted corrugated fence, a wall really, upright and foreboding in the gathering gloom. Above light flickered across an angled rooftop.

He found Sheppard and Crow in the briefing room. Sheppard paced; Crow lounged across an old reclining chair that had seen better days.

Sheppard appeared pissed. "Nice of you to turn up."

Daavid said, "Been up at the observatory."

Sheppard halted, turned, and said, "Find much."

"Some kids making out. Nothing." It felt apologetic. Had there been nothing at all? He'd found a deserted building, wrecked, and a couple making out. They appeared resigned, comfortable with the way things were. Perhaps; "No, not nothing, but I need more time to figure it out."

Crow added his customary, "Right." And Sheppard then said, "Poison. Each of the bodies showed signs of recent and heavy doses of Hemlock. We found remains in the stomachs of the victims."

Crow added, "Kind of ironic, using a poison that starves one of oxygen. A poison that chokes."

Daavid drifted off into another thought.

"You got anything, at all?"

Daavid thought about it. "Possibly. Gelling up here." He tapped his head. "Need to think about it some more."

"Way to go. Keep it to yourself." Sheppard neared, her bald head catching a dance of light in a thin film of sweat. "Share it. Then if we come across information that supports your idea, we can reach a faster resolution."

True, but his thoughts remained half formed, jumbled. "Look, are there any signs of violence on the victims? Any binding marks, bruising, signs of defensive damage?"

Both Sheppard and Crow said, "Nothing."

"Hemlock's in the stomach right."

Sheppard said, "In two."

"Suicides. Ingested the poison deliberately."

Crow laughed. "And who laid their bodies out in a neat row?"

"They'd have had time. Only takes a small amount of poison. They might have sat down and drank it together. The question is why. It's also the answer."

Gasping:

Outside, the sky dimmed. Nightfall would engulf the world in its dark grit-ridden grasp, and soon, people, buildings, and burning street lamps would fade to become dark upon dark shadows, hints of things past. He needed a drink.

Beyond the station's boundary, the crowds he'd seen earlier were thinning. He saw Jam-Jar Joe's across the street, sallow light fighting past grime sheened windows and tattered drapes. A constable's bar. Did he want that? Better establishments frequent the hydroponics district and they lay nearer his home. Drawing his collar higher, he began to hurry along, easily dodging the lessening foot traffic, shop keepers closing up for the night, and the late, leaden faced factory workers trudging home for their supper.

Soon he skirted the Hydro-houses. He heard the gurgle of circulating water, and as he scurried by the loading doors, he saw spears of bright white light slicing out into the murk. A scent of heady loam, citrus, and lavender tickled his nose.

Two streets farther on, he arrived at The Hanging Vine, its faux old-world front, a cobbled together recreation of board and plastic had been worked on extensively, and provided a good if somewhat clichéd facia of a British pub.

Inside, smoke and oil-lamp light added ambience. People thronged the bar and most tables were occupied. Ignoring the crush, he headed toward the rear, hoping to snag a table in the awning tent. Not many people liked it there, the dust managed to sneak in regardless of the tent's attempts to keep it out. Right now, Daavid found he didn't care.

"Daavid Oduba," the voice rang loud over the buzz of the customers. Daavid glanced toward the voice. Henry Gooch, the landlord, wore a huge grin, but before he spoke again, Daavid pointed at the exit and carried on walking. Pointless trying to talk in the noisy bar.

Even in the tent, space came at a premium. One table backed up against the fabric remained free. Daavid moved to take a seat and waited; if he moved, he'd lose it.

His last visit must have been weeks ago; he couldn't remember it being this lively. People had a way of dealing with adversity that he admired. Men played cards, couples cuddled drinks, eyes full of expectation for the evening ahead, and a group of teenagers, perhaps early twenties, laughed on the far side of the tent. Their boisterous nature adding a sense of what? Continuity? The room could have been snatched from any number of places prior to the dust. A snapshot of life.

Henry set down a tray. It held a bottle and two glasses.

"Don't moan, just drink."

Raising an eyebrow, Daavid said, "Surely you haven't missed me that much." He indicated the bottle, the golden liquid within held the reflected lamp light in a warm amber embrace.

"Are you kidding? Look around, place is jumpin', an' I'm happy that's all. Don't get many nights like these anymore."

Pointing at the bottle, Daavid said, "Sure you can spare this. Looks expensive."

"For you, sure. An' it ain't expensive, it's probably priceless. Twenty-year-old spiced rum, let's have some."

Henry poured. The amber liquid swirled and clung against the glass as it settled.

Daavid took his glass and spent a moment savouring the rum's scent. "Henry, you sir, are a gentleman, last of kind."

"I am, ain't I."

Daavid laughed and then took a slow, steady sip. Fire licked at his tongue, sending warmth down into his belly. Aromatic spices danced.

"Henry. Somehow you always know when a guy needs a pick-me-up."

"Part of my job."

A sly grin slipped across Henry's face. "What? You want details?"

"Been a while. And it is the most expensive drink in the house."

"Okay, you got me. It all starts with these four–"

"Mr Oduba?"

As Daavid looked up to see who had addressed him, Henry sighed, annoyed by the interruption. Supressing a smile, Daavid peered up into a slight woman's silhouette. "Yeah?" Something about the woman's shape, the way she held herself, prodded at his memory. "Candida?"

The woman nodded. "I'm sorry to barge in. When you came in, I heard the landlord shout your name and… Well, I wondered if I might have a few moments of your time."

Daavid glanced across at Henry. "Fine Daavid. You show up after weeks, have a juicy case to share, and, well fine, you take the rum and I'll get the young lady a glass. But you're not leaving without talkin,' got it?"

Henry rose from the chair and Candida slid in. As Henry meandered away, Daavid realised he'd never really seen Candida other than in shadow or silhouette. Here the flickering light added a tanned hue to an almond skin. Springy curls fell forward obscuring one eye, which effected a roguish nuance Daavid found appealing.

Suddenly aware of his gaze, he said, "Kam?"

Candida shook her head, "She's gone, left. I doubt I'll see her again."

"Hope it wasn't anything I did."

"No. And anyway; the whole 'making out thing' was really an experiment. A spur-of-the-moment deal."

"Times are when a thing like that can take a hold."

Henry arrived, placed a fresh glass on the table, and poured a large measure before scurrying away.

Candida said, "He seems nice. Known him long?"

"Only after the dust. Thought he might be someone good to cultivate for when the stuff's gone. Don't want to be a constable's consultant once the world's getting better. Fancied a bar job to tied me over for a while. He's a nice guy too."

Candida stared in to her glass. The quiet between them surged and Daavid shifted in his seat and crossed his legs. "Have I said something wrong?"

"No, not really." Snatching her glass up, she shot the rum down in one. Coughed, then said, "Wow. Good stuff."

"The best apparently."

Music started inside the main bar, a mellow jazz number and the pleasant refrains slipped into the tent, counterpoint and sliding riffs lifting the room's mood further.

"Mr Oduba. Is the bottle ours?"

"Looks that way. If it's not, then I guess my first few years as a barman will be spent paying off the bill."

Candida stood, grabbed the bottle and her glass, and said, "In that case can we go someplace else? Somewhere quieter."

Momentarily stunned, Daavid spluttered before saying, "Sure, I guess."

"Someplace where we can watch the sky."

Watch the what? "Being forward, I know, but my place is–"

"Is fine."

Daavid hurried to keep up.

Last Light:

Few ventured out now. Daavid and Candida made easy progress around two blocks of low buildings, having to avoid only late-night dust details and the odd pedestrian.

A flight of dusty stairs came into view. Metal banister switching back on itself twice before it reached a door in the building's side. "We're here," Daavid said, although he felt sure it was obvious.

Candida slid her arm around his elbow, and they took the steps together, a giddy sense of unreality overcoming Daavid as he neared his door.

He opened and stepped back as the door swung outward, stepped in, struck a match, and lit an oil lamp. Turning back to Candida he said, "Welcome. Please follow me."

He led her toward the den and its large window with awning. It gave an unrestricted view of the town nestled across the low hills. However, at night, there'd be little to see. Absently kicking some laundry under a dresser, he reminded himself she'd said somewhere to watch the sky. Odd, but anything to please.

Once inside the large den, he lit several more lamps, placing them so they didn't reflect too much in his window. Still, there was no seeing outside. Perhaps she'd explain. He hoped there'd be more than a little information sent his way. The observatory, the bodies, the whole thing, this woman held the key.

Turning to look at Candida, he saw she'd edged over to an old book case, her attention directed to a small model of Voyager 1. The paintwork wore a coat of age, chips and fades dappled the once tidy colours. The small golden disc shone in the lamplight. He remembered his father persuading him to add a final coat of varnish. The memory hurt.

As he watched, Candida reached out a finger and circled it about the disc, almost reverently.

He broke her thoughts. "An old model, made when I was a kid."

"It's nice. Made me think of all the things we had, all the things we achieved. It's humbling to think that way out beyond the heliopause, a little piece of earth, a piece of us, continues to travel."

In the subdued lighting, Daavid thought he saw a tear edge her cheek.

Fetching the bottle and glasses, he flourished them in the air. "I'll pour."

"Sure." She smiled. "What time is it?"

"Around seven."

"Fine. Once you've filled the glasses can we extinguish the lights? We can slide the couch over to the window and sit staring out at dark."

"Yeah, I guess. But you must promise me something. I want answers, right?"

Smiling again, she simply nodded.

They manoeuvred the couch across the room, Daavid straining his shoulder a little, eventually having to rest it slightly askew. Candida said, "Must be all that action stuff, ducking and diving. You need a massage."

Daavid wondered whether her comment was an offer, but he didn't want to risk offending her. "Just aches and pains of the trade. A good drink and some rest will see me right."

"S'okay, the couch can stay where it is."

"I'm so glad you approve."

Daavid enjoyed the gentle laugh that escaped her lips, and as she sat, he moved around to sit with her.

"Oh no you don't, lamps."

Remembering, he drifted around the room, and extinguished the flickering lights. In the feeble illumination from outside, Daavid stumbled before finding his seat.

"Eyes will acclimate soon."

Candida sounded confident, and Daavid realised that at the observatory she'd have moved around in darkness quite a bit.

Suddenly relaxed, he peered through his window, he felt Candida's hand find his. Her grip was firm, comforting. Should he be more forward, more direct? He suddenly experienced a wave of fatigue, and thoughts of romance melted away. What were they doing, sitting here staring into the dark? One more crazy thing to end a crazy day.

Perhaps he'd fallen asleep or just dozed for a few moments.

Candida's fingers dug deep in his side, released, and dug again. "Wake up, it's starting."

"Wha—"

"Just look out the window."

He sat straighter in his seat, and as Candida snuggled closer, he stared out into the deep dark. Smudges of light, pale flecks in an otherwise velvet view, drew his attention. In the hope of catching something, anything, Daavid leaned forward. "I..."

Slowly, like a cover peeling away from a flashlight, a pale orb blossomed in the sky. The light intensified, its strength appearing to burn through the gloom and grit. *The Sun?* It shouldn't be there, couldn't be there.

The dust filled air remained, immutable, the unexpected light no more or less penetrating than on any other day. Yet Daavid found this unexpected sight uplifting, almost miraculous. Had his life been so empty of wonder, of the sheer joy of an unanticipated light show, that he would allow this giddiness to seep in?

Voices carried up from the street. Followed by laughter. Farther afield a fiddle broke into scratchy melody; people were out there enjoying the moment, living in the now.

Turning toward Candida, he said, "Let's go outside, join the party. Live."

An odd expression crossed her face, but then she smiled and said, "Why not? For a short while anyway."

"Right. Ladies first. I'll bring the bottle, it's not every night the Sun shines."

He noticed Candida glance out of the window, before she said, "No, never."

—————

People danced, laughed in tight groups, and after they'd spun around a few times in the dust riven air, they fell back to huddle under overhanging buildings and shop awnings. Their boisterous joviality flattened by the air carried a tone of release, of unburdened pressure.

Daavid slipped his arm around Candida's waist and she reciprocated. He applied a little pressure, enjoying her body next to his, and as she nestled closer, wondered if he'd see her again. Nowadays relationships tended not to flourish, a product no doubt of the dust and bad lungs. Still, he found the idea attractive.

As they approached a street corner, Candida pulled free, grasped his hand, and began to run. "Come on, I know a place we can go."

He ran after her, dragged along by her hand, and her enthusiasm.

Ahead, people parted to allow them through, and as they crossed a road thick with dust, a petrified park oozed from the gloom. Small, low walled, dust entombed trees surrounding rusted and dilapidated swings. As they entered, Daavid tripped on an old pair of children's shoes.

"Watch your step."

"Tryin'."

Once in the centre, Daavid watched Candida circle a rusted swing before hanging onto one of the supports. She stared at him, cocked her head to one side, and said, "Well."

Unsure, Daavid said, "Huh?"

Candida nodded her head skyward. "That."

Angling his face upward, he fixed his eyes on the pale orb in the sky. It appeared as it always did, a ghostly orb, cloud covered, no dust covered. It might be a little brighter perhaps. "The Sun."

"Daavid, I expected more. Use that mind of yours and look beyond the view."

"Candida, I don—"

"Look again."

The change of her tone almost smacked of annoyance, but perhaps this was important. She had, after all, promised answers.

The orb hung there, weak light as usual, but... Okay it was night so how is there a sun at all? And as he stared, he saw another difference, this orb or radiance, had no black lines, no signs of dust in-fall. It didn't make sense. Had the Sun or Earth moved? Had the dust thinned? Were they coming out of the cloud?

No, it's night, and he had four bodies and a wrecked observatory to account for. And then he knew, knew for certain that whatever this was, it wasn't anything good.

Four dead bodies, possible suicides. A destroyed building, their place of work, and what had Candida said when he'd found her and Kam, "Just making out, well anyone would..."

"You discovered something. The Sun."

"Let's not get ahead of ourselves." She pointed up at the sky. "When I was a little girl, people kept talking about a 'man-in-the-moon'. For a long time, I thought they were being literal. I wasted hours thinking about it, and then searched libraries and the internet. Naturally, I discover pictures of the nearside and captions explaining how the patterns in the craters and seas were in the likeness of a face."

Daavid moved nearer, took hold of one of her hands.

Candida said, "Look, stare as I might, I could never see the pattern, never see what others saw. It drove me nuts. However, it did one good thing. It forced me to look at many an astronomical plate. Moon's surface, Mars, constellations, star and galactic clusters, and nowhere was I able to see shapes or patterns. It's a mental defect, a mild form of agnosia, the occupational therapy was a bitch, but from all those desperate searches came a love of cosmology, a passion that has never left me.

"That, Daavid, is the moon."

Stunned, Daavid turned to look again. It glowed with a brightness he found difficult to accept. Had it been this bright in his youth, when the skies were clear? Laughter and music tugged at his thoughts. *So bright. Reflected sunlight. In real time. So bright that it's years-long absence were now ended in blinding brilliance.*

Dead astronomers, destroyed observatory, experimental sex, that's what Candida had said, "just making out, anyone would".

"Have you known for a while? Why didn't you announce it?"

Candida shrugged. "Does it matter? Look around you. People are happy. Ruining that would have done no good."

"But… the cloud, it should pass right by and we'd sail out to rebuild."

Candida shook her head; a fine cloud of dust fell away. "The dust, we don't know, maybe it has something in it, well we just don't know. The Sun became unstable a few weeks ago, flaring just a little, just enough to get us interested and do some calculations. Right now, there's enough energy and radiation falling on the far side of the world to scour the surface clean."

Daavid clung to her hand, allowing a numbness to claw at his mind. All for nothing. Futile.

Candida said, "There's time for us, time to not be alone."

Silently, they walked back to Daavid's apartment.

Daavid felt their lovemaking held an animalistic energy, an abandonment of the rationale, a last desperate gesture, and he found that gratifying. The fact confronted by this enormity he and Candida rallied against it, refused to wear the mantle of victim.

In the morning, however, as they sat before the wide window watching the dust clouds roil and the upper atmosphere blossom in bright orange and red fire, Daavid realised the universe didn't really care. Victims or not, it moved onward.

A brilliant flash of light limned the deep, dust filled sky. At first, Daavid thought it merely another atmospheric display, but as Candida hugged him tighter, he saw the grey, dust filled sky open to race away over their heads.

For the briefest of moments, he registered a baby blue sky. The sky of his childhood given to him one last time. Perhaps the universe cared after all–

Fire.

One hundred and fifty astronomical units away, cosmic rays danced across a tiny spinning craft. Voyager one tumbled. The high-energy particles surged, etched tiny subatomic dents and holes in an otherwise stained but undamaged disk of gold. As a stray ray of light caught the disk, two outline figures sparkled, then faded.

ROBIN POND

Robin Pond is a Canadian writer and playwright living in Toronto. He is married with three sons and an American grandson who lives in San Francisco (with his parents).

Robin's plays, mainly comedies, have received hundreds of performances and have been published with Eldridge and YouthPLAYS and in several anthologies. One of his full-length plays, **The Retirement Plan**, won a Patron's Pick award at the Toronto Fringe Festival in 2013. This play has now been optioned to be made into a movie and Robin has co-written the screenplay.

Robin's prose fiction reflects eclectic tastes and includes genre fiction—primarily science fiction, mystery, and speculative—as well as more literary efforts. His first mystery novel, **Last Voyage**, was published as an ebook in 2018. And Robin has another science fiction story, **Quantum Entanglement**, scheduled for publication in a U.S. anthology later this year.

CLOSE ENCOUNTER

BY ROBIN POND

Jack looks around the coffee shop anxiously. It's busier than he thought it would be. He circles the room slowly, trying his best not to be obvious while checking out the faces of all the female patrons, especially the few who are sitting alone at tables. Some are attractive candidates, but none appear to be Jillian, although it might be hard to tell. He knows people sometimes don't look much like their profile pictures. He knows this very well since he took considerable care to select a photo of himself which, with a clever mixture of loose-fitting clothing and just the right angle, made him look almost athletic and masterfully concealed his innate pudginess. And his profile picture is now over five years out-of-date, so it's beginning to look better and better. He certainly doesn't consider himself old. Barely thirty. But he is painfully aware of his hairline, the lines around his eyes, the sagging bulge on his waistline, already displaying the warning signs of impending middle-age.

He checks the time on his phone. A few minutes early. He immediately fears appearing too eager. He considers leaving and coming back later, but rejects this notion. What if she spots him leaving? He would look like a fool skulking around like that.

The coffee shop is nearly full, so he decides to grab a table and look busy, in a casual sort of way, to give the appearance of being unconcerned. He chooses one in the far corner, as secluded a spot as he can find, even though the tables are too close together to provide much privacy.

He sits down, back to the wall, and again glances around nervously, sinking below waves of doubt which erode what little confidence he has managed to muster. She's probably had second thoughts and won't show up. It wouldn't be the first time. She probably chose the coffee shop to meet just so she could cruise by, check him out, and then, having seen the greater-than-advertised pudginess, she could simply change her mind and slip away unobserved.

"Jack?"

It's as if she has just appeared in front of his table. "Wow…" He is immediately stunned. She doesn't just look like her picture, she looks far better. Spectacular. Long wavy blonde hair, high cheekbones, slightly pouty pink lips forming a quizzical smile. For a few seconds he stares at her in silence, his mouth sagging open just a bit, his perception bombarded by memory. She looks exactly like Miranda, his long-ago high school crush. The resemblance is staggering.

Recovering belatedly, he scrambles up out of his seat. "Jillian?" Unsure how to greet her, he starts to go in for an embrace, but she remains still, not responding in any way. They end up shaking hands awkwardly. He cringes from his own sense of clumsiness but tries desperately to salvage the situation. "Great, really great, to like meet you in person. I was afraid I might've missed you."

She provides no reaction. "I am sorry if I kept you waiting." She's a bit stiff as they stand facing each other.

"No. Not at all. Just got here myself." He needs to find some way to put her at ease. "Is this table alright?"

She examines the table. "Yes. It seems fine. Quite sturdy." They look at each other for several more seconds.

Finally, he smiles encouragingly. "So should we sit down at it?"

Jillian nods in a deliberate sort of way. "That would appear to be the logical next step. I am interested in proceeding."

They sit down at the table while continuing to look at each other. Jack asks if he can get her anything but she responds, "No. I have no immediate needs."

He launches, haltingly, into rehearsed small-talk. But the gaps in the conversation become painful to him. He desperately doesn't want to screw this up. Realizing he needs to get beyond the banal pleasantries, he takes a deep breath and leans in a bit closer. "You…uh… seem a little nervous…which is totally understandable. I got to admit, I wasn't sure what to expect myself, but now that I've met you…well, it's uncanny, and I hope I don't scare you off by saying this straight out, but you're exactly what I was hoping for."

Her reaction is deadpan. "I know."

He laughs nervously. "Really? It's that obvious?"

But she doesn't appear to be joking. "Yes, my present form is directly guided by your wants. You have easily discernible tastes."

He shrugs almost bashfully. "I guess that's a diplomatic way of saying I'm pretty shallow, and apparently totally transparent."

She still shows no signs of loosening up. "Not in a corporeal sense."

Jack tries several times to get a more interesting conversation going, but with only limited success. Eventually he observes, "You talk kind of weird, if you don't mind me saying. It's not a criticism. It's kind of neat…just…well…a little different. Do I detect an accent?"

"Possibly. I apologize if my responses are inappropriate. This is my first time, and I am not aware of all the proper protocols."

"First time on this site, or any dating site?" he asks.

She tilts her head as if considering. "There are others?"

Jack assures her there are numerous other sites. He lists a number of them before realizing he might appear too knowledgeable in this area. So he quickly adds, "Not that I do a lot of this. Just—you know— now and then. This is my first time too, on the Close Encounters site."

Fortunately Jillian doesn't appear to be put off by his encyclopaedic knowledge of dating sights. "It is a good idea," she agrees. "Most efficient, to fulfill mutual needs in this way."

He shrugs. "Sometimes it works out better than others. But I figure, you've got to just keep putting yourself out there–you know–let chance things happen, and hopefully, some of them'll turn out alright."

"So you believe our getting together to be a serendipitous occurrence?" she asks him.

"Yeah…I guess…Hopefully a good one." He is intent on doing his best to ingratiate himself, hoping for a smile, a lowering of her guard, possibly a softening of her scrutiny.

But she again tilts her head and continues to examine him in that unblinking way of hers. "Sometimes one being's serendipitous occurrence is another being's design."

"Makes sense…I suppose…but either way, I'm glad it's happened…that we've been able to hook up–I mean–get to meet." He glances shyly at her and becomes completely confused. It is more than he had hoped for. Her knowing smile. Dark auburn hair stylishly framing her face, long black lashes flickering above her large green eyes. Abby, his first great passion. It only lasted three weeks before she moved on to some new guy. Jack never completely moved on, and now he is hopeful of having a second chance.

And his optimism soars as she asks, "And what steps do we need to take to complete our hook up?"

He realizes she is actually expecting a reply to this question, so he says, "Well–you know–the usual stuff, I guess. A little talking, find some mutual interests, hang out a bit. See if we click. That sort of stuff."

"Yes, I believe I would like to click. How do we do that?"

Jack shrugs. "I guess it's a chemistry thing."

"We are required to secrete chemicals?"

He laughs. Clearly she is joking. "You pulling my leg?"

But Jillian, once again in the guise of Miranda, actually glances under the table. She looks a bit perplexed. "Would that give you pleasure? I am not familiar with that activity."

Jack laughs awkwardly. "Okay. I get it. You're screwing with me."

"Would you prefer that, or just having me pull your leg?"

He grins. "Yeah, right." He glances over at the counter. "Are you sure I can't get you something?"

Jillian, appearing very serious, replies, "No. I am under certain time constraints. I need us to conclude our business."

"Woah! What business?" Jack suddenly fears he has blundered into an escort service. He knew he should have read through all those terms and conditions on the Close Encounters site rather than merely clicking to proceed. That's the trouble with all the transparency on the internet. It often leads to misunderstanding.

Jillian is patiently explaining something about a transaction between them. Something about the mutual fulfillment of requirements. He interrupts her right there, telling her there might be a terrible misunderstanding, trying his best to not offend her. But when subtlety doesn't seem to be working, he ends up blurting out, "Are you a pro?"

She nods enthusiastically. "Pro? Yes, I am most certainly in favour of this activity." She keeps talking about a mutual transaction satisfying both their needs.

He apologizes for any misunderstanding but emphasizes that if her needs are financial she is out of luck.

Jillian's head tilts yet again. "You mean like a dowry? I am aware of those. But no, that is not necessary. We can be married without financial compensation."

"Woah! Who said anything about getting married?" Now Jack is really concerned. If he was shying away from prostitution, he is now prepared to run as fast as he can away from a lifetime commitment.

But Jillian doesn't seem to understand his reticence. "Is that not why we are here? Your profile stated you are interested in a long-term committed relationship."

"Yeah," Jack assures her. "But everyone says that."

She studies him carefully. "So it is untrue?"

Jack relents. He realizes he is on the verge of ruining his chances with the most alluring woman he has ever met. "Well no…it's not totally untrue…it's just…well…this is kind of crazy." He tries to walk the fine line between ending the relationship and being fully committed to it. "We've barely met and now you're talking marriage. It's a bit sudden. Like maybe we should take a little time to see if we even like each other."

Jillian's countenance appears to soften, bringing Miranda back to mind. "I tried to explain that our connection on Close Encounters was not merely a serendipitous occurrence. You have been selected. Am I not everything you have been looking for?"

"Well...yeah." He admits, "You were–you are–but, to be honest, the talk about long-term commitment right off the bat is a bit off-putting. Kind of a major red flag. But I guess the fact that I'm still here says something. In fact, like I said, aside from the weird conversation...sure–I've got to admit–you do appear to be exactly what I've always dreamed of."

"I know," she tells him with quiet confidence. "You must be attracted to me, because I am able to sense your desires and become them."

"You keep saying that. Do you mean like you're getting a vibe?"

Her head tilts to the side and her appearance shifts again. "Perhaps. I am not familiar with that term. But I am sure you must find me very attractive, Jackie."

She is older, with a rounder face and wavy brown hair. Her lipstick is bright red. A flood of memories. She is just as he remembers her, as a little boy, climbing on to her lap, giving her a hug, secure in the knowledge she will hug him back, stroke his hair, tell him what a good boy he is. He feels a shiver run down his spine. "Ooo...that's the weirdest vibe of all. When you say my name like that, you suddenly remind me of my mother."

She nods. "Then that must be the person to whom you are really attracted."

"Now you're just being disturbing." He stares at her. Her appearance continues to shift. It must be the light in here, he reasons. It's as if she is the embodiment of every woman he has ever been attracted to in his entire life.

"Look, yeah, you're very attractive. Gorgeous in fact. It's just I think we ought to get to know each other, you know? Take our time." He deftly pleads his case, not wanting to give up on her but wary of what he might be getting himself into.

But she continues to press. "I do not have time to wait."

"Why? What's the hurry?"

She lowers her voice, adding a note of urgency. "They are looking for me. I need to blend in, establish a tie to the community. If I do not, they are likely to find me and send me back...or worse."

"Okay, now I'm beginning to get it." Jack is finally able to make sense of this whole situation. "You're like an illegal alien, right?"

"There are legal ones?"

He sighs, knowing it was too good to be true. "So you're just trying to use me as your ticket into the country."

"No," she protests. "I used the portal to get here. I am just trying to use you to blend in and stay."

But he is already getting up out of his chair. "Story of my life. There's always a catch."

Jill scrambles to her feet, trying to stop him from leaving. "Where are you going? I told you I do not require sustenance."

"Look. I'm really sorry." He shakes his head ruefully. "Just looking at you...You don't know how sorry I am. The longer I'm with you, the more alluring you become. But I'm not going to get married just to help you out, you know?"

"But I can provide you with everything you desire."

He senses a note of desperation in her voice but remains adamant. "Maybe. And I'd certainly love to find out. But it wouldn't be fair to either of us to rush into anything. I mean, you don't even know me either, right? And you probably wouldn't like me much once you found out–"

Incorrect," she interrupts. "I already know you as well as you know yourself."

Jack smiles sarcastically. "I very much doubt that."

"I know I am not the only date you have arranged through Close Encounters. You have arranged to meet with two others, one named Beth and one named Laura."

Jack is shocked by the breach in confidentiality. "How the hell'd you find out about that? They're supposed to guarantee privacy. It said so right on the home page. You hack the site or something?"

But Jillian moves in closer. He feels Abby's hot breath on his cheek. "At close proximity I can sense much from you. You have been wondering what the others will be like, and how I might compare.

But I can already tell you, and dispense with you having to meet them."

"What...you like all know each other?" He shifts back away from her but she pursues him.

"There is a certain amount of collaboration." He tries to turn away but she grabs him by the arm. "Believe me, neither of them can satisfy you like I can. Beth's form you will find quite pleasant, but sooner or later, the tentacles will come out. And Laura has difficulty maintaining the human form without secreting gasses. You will find the aroma to be most displeasing."

"So you're saying one's a bitch, and the other one's flatulent? Sounds like maybe somebody's just a wee bit jealous." Despite Jillian's physical appeal, which continues to beguile him, Jack actively looks for a way to end this meeting.

"I am reporting accurately."

He pulls himself free. "Sure you are. But maybe I'd rather find out for myself. Besides, either way, I'm not ready to just up and get married. Like I said, I'm really sorry. I hope it works out for you." He turns his back on her and starts to leave. But she leaps forward and grabs the back of his neck.

"Whoa!" Jack stiffens up and then begins to shake violently. He is impervious to the world around him, experiencing an immense intensity of feeling. Everything. All together. All at once. Suspended in time, not believing he can withstand another millisecond of such an all-encompassing sensation yet never wanting it to end. Every fibre of his body exploding in orgasmic pleasure.

After several seconds, Jillian releases his neck. He almost collapses, but she grabs him and helps him back to his seat. He bends forward, his head resting on his arms which are curled up on the table.

A barista, a thin man with a green apron and large toothy smile, approaches their table and offers samples of the sponge cake. "I do not require your food." Jillian firmly tells him. Jack weakly waves him away.

After a few more moments, Jack sits back up. He asks hoarsely, "What the hell was that?"

Jillian is back to being Abby. She gives him a knowing smirk. "Did you not find it extremely pleasurable?"

"It was incredible." He admits. "Unbelievable. I never expected… especially on a first date. But I don't get how you can do that through– you know–just touching my neck."

"All human sensation is experienced in the brain. This is just a more direct approach, tapping directly into the brain-stem."

"You got like magic buzzers attached to your fingers or something?"

"It is neural stimuli." She tells him matter-of-factly. "On my planet we interact primarily through bio-feedback mechanisms."

"Your planet?"

She again tilts her head. "I thought you understood. I am an alien."

And Jack, who is admittedly not the quickest on the uptake, finally comprehends. "That type of alien?"

She continues to explain. "The Close Encounters website has been set up by those of us who have made the journey to Earth so we might integrate into your society."

Jack's natural cowardice again kicks in. "Oh, hell." He is still a bit woozy from his recent experience but struggles to stand up. "This was already too weird for me when I thought you were just running an immigration scam. I've really got to go."

But Jillian reaches across the table and, placing both her hands on Jack's shoulders, she firmly pushes him back into his seat. "Sit down, Jackie. Do not be rude."

"Stop being my mother!" He protests weakly.

She leans forward. "But that is just the point. I can be anyone you want me to be. And as your tastes change over time, my appearance will change to accommodate them. I can provide you with everything you desire, not just once but continuously."

Jack rubs his neck thoughtfully. "Yeah, I know. You gave me a hell of a demonstration."

"That was only a small sample. I can do much better than that."

He looks at her. She is, at one and the same time, every woman he has ever loved or ever desired. "Better? Really?"

"Yes." She assures him. "Unfortunately you have not really had many encounters with women, so initially I did not have much experience to draw from."

He glances around nervously at the people sitting at the surrounding tables, but fortunately no one seems to notice. "Hey, keep your voice down."

But she informs him she is able to surround the table with a perception block so most of the others in the coffee-shop don't notice them.

He nods, readily accepting all this information as if none of it were extraordinary, merely thinking to himself he didn't need to worry earlier about finding a secluded table so they could have some privacy.

"And with every meld it will get better." She tells him. "I cannot wait to experience the full weight of your passion."

Jack thinks about this, all the while being further beguiled by the array of lovely creatures he sees before him. "But how are you experiencing it? I thought this was all just for me, to get me to agree to help you."

Jillian smiles. It is Abby's knowing smirk. "You still do not completely understand. The bio-feedback loop is complete. I experience exactly what you experience."

Slowly he becomes convinced. "So let me get this straight. You know all my secrets, and you still want to be with me. You're guaranteed to always be the woman of my dreams. And every time we're, like, together, I'm sure of pleasing you just as much as you're pleasing me?"

She gets up and walks around the table, positions herself behind him, and places her hands gently on the back of his neck. "Yes. Let me show you."

Jack starts to object. "What? Here?"

She gently rubs her hands over the back of his head and neck, reminding him of the perception block, telling him, "It is fine. Just the two of us. No one will notice us. No one else in the entire universe. Just relax. Let yourself go. Your mind rising to my mind, consciousness to consciousness..."

Jack has a sudden image of an old Star Trek episode, but she whacks him on the side of the head, telling him to focus. "Feel it. Own it. Be it. Two together as one." They both stiffen and start to shake. All the colours of the rainbow more intense than perceptually possible. All light. All sound. Movement–soaring, falling, all in one. All energy focused down into a single point of origin and then exploding out in an ecstasy of pure feeling.

Jack jumps to his feet screaming, "Oh…my…God!"

The two of them are suspended there, over a chair in a coffee-shop, shuddering in unison. Finally, they sink down, sagging against each other.

"You really think you can improve on that?" Jack asks breathlessly.

"Every time there will be improvement." She replies confidently.

Jack falls at her feet. "Marry me!"

Smiling radiantly, she lifts him back up and they embrace passionately. "I thought you would never ask." She murmurs as he holds her tightly.

They sit back down at the table. He again asks her if she would like a coffee or something to eat but she assures him she already has everything she wants.

Jack smiles at his new love. "I still can't believe it. It's kind of crazy, you know? It all happened so fast. But I really think it'll work. The connection is undeniable. We make a great team."

"Yes we do." She readily agrees. "And I promise I will not abandon you. I will be right by your side when you give birth."

Jack chuckles, trying not to be condescending but realizing she still has a lot to learn. "You've got that a little bit backwards, dear. It's the woman who gives birth…at least here on Earth it is."

Jillian responds with her characteristic head tilt. "Yes, you do seem to have firmly entrenched gender stereotypes. On my planet we are much more androgynous."

"Whoa! You saying you're like…really a dude?"

"No…not exactly. I am saying the distinctions, the gender roles, are not as meaningful for my kind."

He smiles. "Yeah, sweetie, but they're kind of important to me. Besides, you're on earth now, and so…when in Rome, you know?"

She clearly doesn't understand the reference to Rome, but explains it doesn't really matter where they are. "You will still have to give birth to our babies."

Jack shakes his head adamantly. "I really don't think so. At the very least, we ought to discuss it."

"It is too late for discussion, Jackie." She is his mother again. Her bright red mouth forms a little pout as she quietly explains to him the way things are. "I have already laid my eggs in your abdomen."

With the perception block in place, no one in the coffee shop can hear Jack scream.

DAVE STEINMAN

Dave Steinman is a Crystal nomi-
nated commercial copy writer and
voice artist currently residing in beautiful British Columbia on Canada's
west coast. After 25 years in the radio
business, he was surprised to discover
that he could write something longer
than 30 seconds that didn't end with
the phrase "Hurry...sale ends tomorrow." This is his third published short
story, and he is currently working on
his first full length novel.

I'M TELLING YOU FOR THE LAST TIME

By DAVE STEINMAN

The first time the world ended, he was caught completely off guard. After that, it was his responsibility to make sure it never happened again.

Now, if you're having a hard time following what that means, it's alright. It's not supposed to make total sense. But this is what happens when you mess with time. Did I not mention time travel was involved? I guess the assumption was you'd already figured that out. So, yes... time travel! Oh, it's a real thing, just like all those movies said. Most of them got it wrong, by the way...except for a little seen Bollywood musical that came surprisingly close. No one is quite sure how that happened. All we know is it's possible. But just like the enduring popularity of Neil Diamond, no one can figure out why. The whole process revolves around a certain piece of alien technology...sorry... aliens are real too...discovered in Roswell, New Mexico. Cliché? Sure...but absolutely true nonetheless. Anyway, back to the end of the world.

It starts with one Lurgo Wix. A person, we might add, of questionable reputation. Actually, to say he is a person is a bit of a stretch. Lurgo Wix is not human at all, although he does possess one particular talent humans are quite good at. Lurgo Wix can lie like nobody's business…which is quite remarkable considering he is from Bellaxitor, a planet revered as a paragon of virtue and decency across the universe. Now, how he came to possess this capacity for all manner of fibs, untruths, prevarications, and utter bullshit while growing up in that environment is a mystery. Perhaps it's because in addition to being virtuous and decent, Bellaxitor is also well known for being exceedingly milquetoast and, well, appallingly drab and awful…things Lurgo Wix was most definitely not. It may also explain how he came to be in the vicinity of Roswell, New Mexico during the first week of July, 1947.

While it's true a spaceship did indeed crash land in the desert outside of Roswell, a fact not really in dispute among those who are in the know about such things, what most are not aware of is there was more than one. Some hours before the actual crash, Lurgo Wix, in a craft he had liberated from the Bellaxitor City Spaceport, had been forced to make an emergency landing on Earth when he spilled his drink on the ship's control console, causing all manner of warning lights and bells to go off. A hurried consultation of the ship's operating instructions made him quickly realize he was hopelessly out of his element. After pushing a bunch of random buttons in the vain hope one of them would save his Bellaxitorian bacon, he threw up his hands in defeat and accidentally hit a switch just behind his command couch labelled "in case of emergency".

One important thing to know about Lurgo Wix is not only is he an unabashed liar, thief, and grifter extraordinaire, he is also one the of the luckiest S.O.B.'s you could ever meet. The switch tripped the ship's auto-pilot, which proceeded to guide the stolen craft to a soft landing in that now legendary area of the New Mexico desert.

As he sat there waiting for the ship to repair itself, Lurgo took time to survey his surroundings. Since he was now stranded in the middle of the nowhere, it didn't take very long, and he became bored very quickly. The ship's computer estimated 4 hours, local planetary time, to affect repairs. So, with time to waste, Lurgo decided to make his way to the cargo area to look for anything useful he might be able to trade or sell on his next trip to the Galactic Hole, which was a sort of interstellar flea market where various bandits, thieves, and all manner of unpleasant beings sold their many ill-gotten wares, no questions asked.

He had nearly completed his inventory of purloined booty, which included a number of items he was sure would fetch a decent price, when a strange keening sound coming from outside attracted his attention. Poking his head out of the rear of the ship, he was very surprised to discover a large, threatening fireball headed directly toward his present location. He had just enough time to close the cargo door before it impacted the earth and exploded in a blooming cloud of fire, smoke, and ash a short distance away.

Now, for the most part, Lurgo was not a particularly inquisitive type, especially when something potentially catastrophic and life threatening was occurring nearby. His normal modus operandi was to run...very quickly and usually in the opposite direction of the problem. It was this flight, not fight, instinct that saved him on numerous occasions, including the time a jealous husband of a Bellaxitorian society matron caught them in a rather...well...delicate situation.

This time, however, curiosity got the better of him, and he eventually decided to venture outside the safe confines of his still inoperable ship to see just what caused the ruckus. This was his first mistake. The United States Army had also shown up, en masse, to do the same thing. If he'd stayed inside, they wouldn't have had the slightest clue there was a second spaceship in the vicinity. The computer on Lurgo's stolen craft had put the ship into stealth mode the moment it landed, rendering it invisible to any stray passersby. It's a safety measure, designed for situations specifically like accidentally landing on an insignificant planet in a backwater part of a minor galaxy that only recently progressed to the internal combustion engine. Earth, in this case.

Now, if Lurgo had paid more attention in school instead of trying to invent new ways to cheat his classmates out of their lunch money, he might have known this. But he didn't. You see, while he may have been a con man par excellence, Lurgo Wix sadly lacked when it came to things mechanical and electronic. To put it bluntly...he was no rocket scientist. Like many of us, he knew how to make things go, like a carelessly unlocked spaceship that could do zero to bubble warp in the blink of an eye, but he had no clue exactly why. The question never came up, so it was never an issue.

Lurgo keyed the cargo door of the ship open for a better look and immediately regretted it. He was summarily greeted by a rather large group of soldiers, carrying an equal number of standard issue rifles, all aimed directly at him. Shortly thereafter, Lurgo and the ship, which he had been forced to uncloak, were both taken from the scene and held in an undisclosed facility until his eventual transfer to Area 51. In time, he convinced his captors that he was no threat to anyone's national security, nor was he the tip of the spear in some secret extraterrestrial invasion plan.

Earth, he told them, was neither strategically located, nor advanced enough to be of any use to any other race in its immediate proximity. They were, to use a local euphemism, "yokels". The galactic equivalent of the Beverly Hillbillies... they meant well, but were, for the most part, believed to be dumber than a sack of hammers. They questioned him about the other ship, the one that crashed and burned the night they picked him up, but he had no idea who or what they were, or what they were doing in the general vicinity of this planet. Lurgo's ship, on the other hand, contained a veritable treasure trove of alien devices, some of which proved to be very useful to his captors.

To Earth scientists of the day, the devices found in the back of the ship seemed light years beyond normal human comprehension. It was comparable to cavemen trying to figure out how to use a microwave. But even the dumbest caveman can turn on a microwave if he knows which button to push...and Lurgo Wix was no caveman. Sensing there was a deal to be had, and fearful for his own skin, he struck a bargain with the people who eventually become his employers. Lurgo offered to show them how each of the gadgets worked, but only under one condition. They would only be allowed to present him with one per year.

Time passed, and he spent the rest of the 20th century, and into the new millennium, demonstrating, one at a time, the devices from his ship. Other than "Gadget Day", as he took to calling it, there really wasn't a whole lot else for him to do. Even though his captors came to eventually understand he was no threat, they still couldn't have him wandering around interacting with people. Someone was bound to get curious. So he watched a lot of TV, and played a lot of board games with his guards. He got really good at Monopoly, although that was only because he cheated.

Over time, the alien hardware began to dwindle down, and he became fearful that without something to present to his current bene-factors, they would have no further use for him, and that would be that. It was about this time they came to him with a device that he knew all too well, mainly because it had a heinous reputation throughout the galaxies as the most ridiculous invention ever...a colossal waste time and energy. It was so reviled it didn't even have a proper name. It took the equivalent of 12 earth years and 17 trillion dollars to perfect. And what did this glorious piece of technological legerdemain actually do? It found missing socks. Needless to say, the scientists, and there were more than a few who were part of the process, were immediately banished to a remote corner of the universe and made to live out the rest of their existence watching re-runs of a mediocre sitcom called "Hey, That's My Shoetree," and listen to Dixieland music, which isn't just reviled on earth.

Picking up the loathsome contraption, Lurgo dutifully pointed it at the far corner of his living quarters, located in a nondescript yet still heavily guarded section of Area 51. As he expected, the machine began to beep and boop, which he knew would then be followed by a voice giving out the various locations of any missing socks within a 500-foot radius. What happened next was totally unexpected.

Instead of the harsh, mechanical voice originally programmed in by the machine's creators, another reason why the thing was universally hated, Lurgo and the assembled group were instead greeted with a rather soothing yet faintly patronizing female voice which intoned the following message:

"Attention. Your world has been designated for removal and destruction. If you wish to stop this process, please proceed through the portal. You have five minutes to make your decision, after which, the portal will close. Thank you and have a pleasant day."

The portal referred to by the voice shimmered into view at the spot Lurgo pointed the machine.

"Well, that's new," he said placidly.

Indeed, it was. Because for whatever reason, be it the Terran atmosphere, some anomaly the ship had flown through on the way to Earth, or just pure cosmic flukery, the loathsome sock-finder had been transformed into a sort of doomsday alarm clock, complete with time travel reset capabilities.

So, there they stood: Lurgo Wix, Dr. Eugene Melnik, the scientist currently tasked with witnessing and cataloguing the "Gadget Day" device, and Agent Robert Keen, who was in charge of security for The Wix Project for "The Company", a mysterious off the books government agency overseeing...well, let's just say "lots of different things" and leave it at that. The three of them were, to say the least, dumbfounded by what just occurred. The scientist and the government agent because of the obvious implications for the future, and Lurgo because he couldn't fathom what was going on at all. He was pretty sure there had been no upgrades to the sock finder since its initial invention, the reasons being mentioned before. So, what was this end of the world, shimmering portal to somewhere nonsense? Agent Keen was the first to broach the subject.

"Wix, what the hell is going on here? You said this thing was supposed to find lost socks," he shouted, pointing at machine. "Now it's telling us the world's going to be destroyed and we have to go through there to stop it?"

"It would appear that way, yes," Lurgo replied hesitantly. "Look, I'm as clueless about this as you are. I've used this thing lots in the past and it never did this, not once."

Keen appeared unimpressed by Lurgo's explanation, and turned to the only person possessing even a remotely scientific mind in the room. "Dr. Melnik, what do you make of this?"

"I have no idea," he replied.

"Well that's just great!" Keen shot back. "It's the end of the world as we know it and I feel freakin' fine!"

"Ooh, I love that song," Lurgo said excitedly.

Keen gave Lurgo a dirty look and turned once again to Dr. Melnik, who was not only the smartest person in the room, but also the most rational. Melnik pondered the situation for a few moments and then appeared to come to a decision.

"Well, if this machine is telling us the world is going to end and that we can stop it by going through that portal, then I say we have to go."

It was then Lurgo Wix decided, without any prodding or threat of bodily harm, to do something good for someone else besides himself.

"Then let me do it," he said suddenly. "I feel kind of responsible for this whole situation, so the least I can do is try and fix it."

"Oh, hell no! You are not going through there by yourself Wix," Keen shouted.

"C'mon, Keen," Lurgo shot back. "What do think I'm going to do? Run away? You've got my ship. I can't go anywhere, and even if I could, why would I? This is a pretty sweet setup, in case you had forgotten. I'd be a fool to give it up," he said none too convincingly.

"Save it! I will be going with you to make sure you do what you're supposed to, and that you then return to this room where you belong. And since I don't know how much time that thing is going to give us, I suggest we get moving."

Lurgo was mildly relieved Keen was going with him. His momentary act of decency had been quickly followed by a sudden dread that he had no idea what he was getting himself into, so Keen's paranoia with setting him loose on the free world had actually worked in his favour. Because despite being locked up in Area 51 for decades, he had actually grown quite fond of these people and had no wish to see their world end, no matter how backward and primitive he thought it was. He found them to be, by and large, a decent and productive species that should have the opportunity to grow and become part of the larger interstellar community. To have this civilization end now would be a tremendous waste. Besides, he was quite keen on getting out of this complex and seeing some of the world, and if it meant that he had to do a little work, like saving the planet, then so be it.

"Fine by me," Lurgo said. "I didn't want to do this by myself anyway."

Keen turned to Dr. Melnik. "Doctor, since we have no idea about where this thing is going to take us, and how long we'll be away, you're going to have to inform the company about where we've gone and why. Of course, if we don't come back, then it's not going to make much difference because we've failed and the world's going to end." His final words hung in the air between them for a few moments before the Doctor responded.

"Of course, Agent Keen, I understand." He looked thoughtfully over at Lurgo. "Lurgo, you and I have known each other for a long time, and I just want to say that in that time, I've come to realize something."

"What's that Doc?" Lurgo replied.

"You are by far the most irresponsible, shiftless being I have ever met, on this world or any other. Now, that being said, please do your best to save my planet. It's the only one I have."

"Will do, Doc," Lurgo said, clapping him hesitantly on the shoulder. "Okay Keen, let's get this show on the road. I wanna get back in time to watch the Wheel."

And with that, they stepped through the portal to their fate on the other side. They emerged into a large, empty hotel room overlooking a busy downtown area that looked to Robert Keen like midtown Manhattan. The patronizing voice that had previously informed them of Earth's impending destruction resumed.

"Welcome Agent Robert Keen of Earth and Lurgo Wix of Bellaxitor. Congratulations on a wise decision to save this planet. You have been brought to this room to avoid disruption of this briefing as, according to our records, it will not be occupied for another 48 hours. Here are the details. On August 14th, 2020, at approximately 12:27pm, Eastern Standard Time, Donald J. Smith, a network technician employed at a Manhattan, New York data centre, will accidentally send out a signal to the Calipsigyan Planetary Demolition Company to destroy this planet. You must stop Mr. Smith before he completes his task, or your planet will cease to exist in 7 earth days. It is currently 9:12am, Monday, August 14th, 2020. You have approximately 3 hours to complete your task, at which time you will be able to return to your own timeline. You will find further details in this room's desk. Thank you and have a pleasant tomorrow…or not."

They discovered a small portfolio in the desk with their names dutifully printed on the front. Inside were the address and company name employing Mr. Smith, a photo they assumed was him, and instructions on where he could be located at the time the voice indicated. Aside from that, it appeared that they were on their own.

Now, you may be wondering…how could a simple computer network technician like Donald Smith manage to send a signal to an interstellar demolition company? And the answer would be… pure dumb luck. Donald Smith had been spending most of his lunch hours during the preceding few months trying to concoct an algorithm that would allow him to hack a satellite uplink and get free TV. He had, up until the morning of August 14th, been demonstrably unsuccessful. And it would have continued that way if it were not for the feminine charms of one Bethany Sexsmith, also employed at the same location. To say he was smitten with her was putting it mildly. Any excuse to visit her workstation, no matter how lame, was a good one as far as he was concerned. So, when Bethany made her way past him that day and bent over to pick up the pen she had just dropped, naturally his attention was drawn away from the keyboard he was typing away at. It was just enough of a distraction to allow him to input two particular, but significant keystrokes into his algorithm.

After he finished ogling Bethany's ample backside, he returned to his keyboard. If he was successful, a notice he had rigged up on his phone would alert him he was now a bona fide satellite TV pirate. He waited patiently, but, as had happened many times before, he got nothing. Disappointed, he put the algorithm aside one more time and got up from his desk to see if the lovely Bethany needed his help. What Donald Smith wasn't aware of was this time, his algorithm had worked. Just not in the way he had planned it. Instead, the signal from his computer reached an orbiting communications satellite and caused a short, which then rerouted that signal to a relay station the Calipsigyan Planetary Demolition Company recently installed in the Kuiper Belt. Eventually, it reached the company's head office, where an order for the demolition of Earth, 3rd planet in Sol system, was processed and approved. Once the order was approved, the only way it could be reversed was by a direct request from whoever sent it. No exceptions. That would have been impossible in this case anyway because the person who sent it had no idea what he had done, and wouldn't have known how to fix the problem even if he was aware there was one, which, of course, he was not.

And so, Earth seemed doomed to a rather inglorious and messy end, unless of course Lurgo Wix and Robert Keen could get to Donald Smith before he hit send.

At the very same time the two time travelers were on their way to prevent Donald Smith from keystroking the planet out of existence, Jeff Ray Peavey was reluctantly preparing to re-enter the workforce proper, having recently left his job at a local t-shirt kiosk. In actual fact he was asked to leave after he had pointedly and very loudly refused to print what seemed to him like the one millionth grumpy cat meme shirt for a somewhat bewildered suburban soccer mom.

After taking some time to consider his current dire circumstances, he decided to swallow his pride and go to work, at least in the interim, for "the man", which in this case was whoever was behind the want-ad in the previous day's New York Times. Someone was searching for young professional men and women to staff a data centre in mid-town Manhattan. It didn't go into specifics about what the job entailed… just that it required some degree of computer expertise, discretion, and a "can-do" attitude. Jeff Ray figured this sounded as good as anything else he was destined to find, so why not?

He arrived at the address specified just before noon. A drab, non-descript three story office building that had seen better days just off 5th Avenue. The lobby was staffed by a lone security guard, reading what appeared to be one of those yellow and black "guides for dummies" books. If Jeff Ray had bothered to take a closer look at the title, he might have had second thoughts about continuing on his way. The book was called "*So You're Stranded on Earth: Now What? An Alien's*

Guide to Surviving on the 3rd Rock from the Sun." Jeff Ray paid the guard no attention, however, and proceeded to the elevator at the end of the lobby.

The building directory indicated the company in the want-ad was located on the 4th floor, which seemed odd considering he was pretty sure this building had only three stories. What was even odder was the elevator had no 4th floor button...just one with a mysterious pattern that looked like a combination of Prince's symbol and a Mobius strip. Throwing caution to the wind, he punched the not-the-fourth-floor button and waited for the elevator to take him to his destiny...or his next pay cheque. At this point, he was indifferent to either.

The elevator doors opened onto a fairly elaborate reception area with lots of glass and wood and a few plants scattered here and there. Behind the desk sat an attractive yet very business-like receptionist. On the wall behind her hung what could only be the company name: NTSH DATA

The name was accompanied by the logo he had seen on the elevator floor button. He approached the desk confidently but with a nagging suspicion something about this wasn't quite right.

"Good day, sir," the receptionist intoned. "How can I help you?"

"Uh, hi," Jeff Ray said hesitantly. "I'm here about your ad in the Times...for the data entry position?"

"Certainly, Mr..."

"Peavey," he replied. "Jeff Ray Peavey."

"Mr. Peavey. Please have a seat and someone will see you shortly."

He took a seat in one of the plush chairs to the right of the desk, and set about patiently waiting. It was about this time Lurgo Wix and Robert Keen arrived in the lobby, still arguing about how they were going to get into the heart of the data centre where they were supposed to locate Donald Smith. Keen suggested since he actually worked for the government, even if it was in the past, they pull the "in the interest of National Security" card and just barge in. Lurgo, however, suggested they not draw attention to themselves to avoid disrupting the timeline any more than they absolutely had to.

"Look Keen," Wix said as they made their way toward the elevators. "We can't just go running in guns blazing. A job like this requires a lighter touch. You know...stealth, cunning...a certain amount of bullshit?"

"Well, if there's anyone who knows about that, it's you," Keen shot back.

Lurgo ignored the remark. "Trust me. I've done this kind of thing hundreds of times. Let me handle it."

"Alright," a clearly exasperated Keen replied. "I'll let you take your shot. But if it doesn't work, then we do it my way."

"Man, how did your world survive all this time with guys like you running the show?"

Upon arriving at the 4th floor lobby, Lurgo strode confidently up to the receptionist's desk, thoroughly prepared to turn his legendary charm up to the max.

"Good day, gentlemen, how may I help you today?" she said brightly as they approached. Jeff Ray Peavey, who had been idly perusing an ancient People magazine he found in the reception area, quickly glanced up to see who else had happened along on this already peculiar day.

"Oh, no darling," Lurgo replied in his most unctuous and obsequious voice. It was one he had perfected from watching 60 plus years of B-movies. "It's not you who can help us. It is we who can help you. My name is Fein...Sidney Fein...and this is my associate, Mr Weintraub. We represent Miracle Pictures. Perhaps you've heard of us? You know...if it's a hit, it's a Miracle!"

The receptionist seemed nonplussed and thoroughly unimpressed by Lurgo's line of patter. Keen merely looked sick as Lurgo chuckled at this own joke.

"Anyway, sweetheart, we were out scouting locations and we happened by this fabulous building. The architecture is simply stunning, don't you think Saul?" Lurgo smiled an oily smile in Keen's direction, who remained stone faced. He turned back to the receptionist and continued. "Anyway darling, I wonder if we could just get a look at the interior of the rest of the building? You know, so we can get the 'lay of the land' so to speak."

Peavey observed the two newcomers from his perch in the waiting area and immediately had a strange urge. *I should follow these two no matter where they go.* He had no idea why, but the moment he laid eyes on Lurgo Wix, he couldn't shake the feeling that they had met before…somewhere, sometime…he just couldn't put his finger on it. What he was probably experiencing was some residual leftover from the various trips through time he was due to take with Lurgo in the service of saving the planet, even though none of them had even happened yet. Time travel has a funny way of affecting the memory, much like Mexican food can affect your digestion. You don't think about it at the time, but afterward, the memory of it can linger for a long time.

The receptionist smiled sweetly at Lurgo and Keen. "Certainly sir. Just go through that door and down the hall. Someone will take care of you once you're inside."

Lurgo was a little taken aback by the ease with which his scheme had worked, but he chalked it up to his fabulous charm, and pulled Keen toward the door.

"Well, thank you, darling. We'll be sure to give you a credit on the picture. What did you say your name was?"

"I didn't," she replied coldly.

The tone of her voice made Lurgo stop for a second and consider whether this was still a good idea, but Keen shoved him through the door and into the adjoining hallway.

"See," Lurgo said. "I told you it would work. Easy as *blatka!*"

Keen was not impressed. "Yeah, a little too easy if you ask me."

"Ah, you worry too much," Lurgo said as they made their way down the hallway.

"What the hell is *blatka*, anyway?

"A Bellaxitorian delicacy. You should try it some time."

"I'll pass," Keen said.

"Suit yourself," Lurgo replied.

"Just keep your eyes open. The sooner we find this Smith guy the better. I've got a bad feeling about that receptionist."

He was right to be worried. After they had passed through the door, she picked up the phone on her desk, and told the person on the other end. "It's Peel. I've got two on their way to the pit. Yes, I agree. Thank you." She was about to place the phone back when she noticed the door to the hallway still ajar, and the gentleman who had been waiting for his job interview was no longer there. She spoke again into the phone.

"Actually, make that three. And let me know when they're taken care of."

Lurgo and Keen, meanwhile, had just disappeared through a side door at the end of the hall, quickly followed by Peavey. They were all about to enter into a situation that would change their lives forever.

The door exited onto a small balcony with stairs leading down to the main complex floor. However, when Keen took a closer look at what was going on down below, he realized where they were. He had seen this type of setup many times before. The mammoth wall of screens at the far end and the numerous workstations on the floor told him this was not some random call centre. It was a Company site, probably set up for monitoring any and all types of electronic traffic. Home and cell phone calls, e-mail, fax, Morse code…everything. These types of stations were set up after 9/11 to monitor terrorist chatter, but this one was way beyond anything he had been privy to. Then he remembered they were more than a decade into the future, and it all made sense…sort of. He also realized something else.

"Oh man," he said to no one in particular. "We're in big trouble."

Before Lurgo could ask why, Jeff Ray Peavey came through the door behind them and immediately regretted it. The scene in front of him was like something out of a James Bond movie.

"Oh this is not good!" he said slowly.

"Who the hell are you?" Keen said to the stranger.

"I'm Jeff Ray Peavey. I was here to apply for a job. I'm beginning to think I should have stayed in bed."

Lurgo turned to Jeff Ray with a puzzled look. "Do I know you?" he asked.

"That's funny," replied Peavey. "I was going to ask you the same thing."

"Hey, I don't mean to interrupt old home week here but we've got to find Donald Smith before the Company's goons show up," Keen said with more than a hint of exasperation.

"The Company?" Wix said worriedly. "What have they got to do with this?"

"Take a look around genius," replied Keen. "This is a black site. And that receptionist you think you charmed the panties off was probably on the phone ten seconds after we went through the door...which means we've got about thirty seconds to find this guy and stop the end of the world before they come for us."

Jeff Ray suddenly got a sick, yet familiar feeling in the pit of his stomach. "Wait, what does he mean 'the end of the world'?"

"I'll explain it to you later," Wix replied quickly. "Right now, we need to find this guy." He showed Jeff Ray the picture of Donald Smith provided by the sock-finder.

Now, I've said it before, but I think it bears repeating. Lurgo Wix was indeed one of the luckiest S.O.B.'s you would ever want to meet. Because it so happened the person he and Keen were looking for, one Donald J. Smith, was seated at a work station just below them. But that wasn't who Lurgo saw first. No, the person who caught his eye was none other than Bethany Sexsmith, about to make her way past the soon to be momentarily distracted Mr. Smith. Lurgo followed her for a few seconds, before casting his eye up ahead, where he spied their target beavering away at his keyboard.

The three of them rushed from the balcony down to the floor. Just before they reached Smith's workstation, they saw his head turn to watch the girl of his dreams stroll by, all the while keeping his fingers busy on his keyboard. As Bethany Sexsmith prepared to bend over to retrieve her wayward pen, the Company agents sent by the receptionist suddenly burst through the upper door. She turned and screamed, as did Donald J. Smith...and not in a manly way, either. Much to the horror of Wix and Keen, his finger's never left the home row of his computer keyboard. Something came over Jeff Ray Peavey...an inexplicable feeling that he must stop this guy from doing any more typing or all would be lost. What prompted him to lunge at Smith and knock him from his chair isn't clear. It could be the memory thing mentioned earlier, but it could also be just another facet of Lurgo Wix's unbelievable luck. Whatever the reason, the moment the two of them tumbled to the floor, the shimmering portal Keen and Wix had stepped out of in the mid-town hotel room re-appeared at the far end of the station floor.

"Mission complete," the slightly patronizing female voice intoned from the sock-finder.

"Hey, we did it!" Lurgo exclaimed. "We saved the world, Keen!"

Jeff Ray Peavey wasn't so ebullient. "That's all well and good guys, but who's supposed to save us?" He cocked his head toward the phalanx of Company agents currently headed their way. Luckily for all of them, they were in the presence of perhaps the most skillful being in the universe when it came to squirming out of seemingly hopeless situations, that being one Lurgo Wix of Bellaxitor, lately of Earth.

Wix thought for a brief second. "Keen…give me your gun."

"What? Are you crazy? I'm NOT giving you my gun."

"Keen! I need it so I can take the both of you hostage."

"Hostage? What are you talking about?"

"Look, we need to get over to the portal, right?" Keen nodded. Lurgo smiled, "So, I'm going to tell them you two are my hostages, and we're going to slowly move toward it until we're close enough to make the jump."

Keen looked puzzled. "Why don't I just keep the gun and take YOU hostage?"

"Because you look like them," Lurgo shot back. "They won't shoot if they think one of their own is in danger."

Jeff Ray, still thoroughly confused by everything happening around him, decided it was an opportune time to butt in.

"So, what am I supposed to do while all this is going on?" he asked Lurgo.

"Stand beside him and play the second hostage. All you have to is look scared."

"Not a problem. What happens when we get to that portal thingy?" he asked.

Lurgo thought for a second. "How old were you in 2007?" he asked.

"15," Jeff Ray said. "Why?"

"Any regrets since then?"

"Quite a few, actually," he replied.

"Well, then this will be your chance to fix all that."

Lurgo turned back to Keen, who reluctantly handed the alien his gun. Wix smiled triumphantly and clapped his hand on Keen's shoulder.

"Don't worry, Dude. I've done this kind of thing lots of times. Well…maybe not lots but…" He left the thought hanging as he pulled Keen and Jeff Ray up from the floor and called out to the agents closing in on their position.

"All right, all of you back off or both of them get it!" He waived the gun in the air for emphasis, and then whispered to Keen. "Safety's on, right?"

"Oh, hell yeah," Keen retorted.

They began to inch their way toward the waiting portal at the back of the data centre, Keen and Peavey in front with their hands in the air, Lurgo behind them with the gun poking out between them. They reached the portal just in time for the device voice to call out once again.

"This portal will disengage in 10 seconds. If you would like to wait for the next scheduled engagement, another will occur in approximately 12,000 years…give or take." The voice began counting down.

"I'm really beginning to hate that thing," Keen said.

"You and me both, pal!" Lurgo shot back. "Okay, on the count of three, we jump!"

"Wait…in there?" Jeff Ray Peavey exclaimed.

Lurgo ignored him and waited for the device to reach four before beginning his own count.

"3…2…1…Now!"

The three of them turned and leaped through the portal, instantly vanishing in full view of the entire stunned room. They stepped out the other side back into the room in Area 51, none the worse for wear. The first person to greet them on their return was Dr. Melnik.

"Hey, Doc," Lurgo cheerfully said. "Long time no see."

"Long time?" the Doctor quizzically replied. "You've only been gone a few seconds."

"Oh yeah? Cool!"

"How long were you actually on the other side, Lurgo?

"About three hours," he replied.

"Really? But who is this?" he said, pointing to the mysterious third party now in the room with them.

Jeff Ray extended his hand. "Jeff Ray Peavey. Nice to meet you."

Melnik looked uncomprehendingly at Lurgo.

"Collateral damage," he said. "I'll explain later. Right now, I need to decompress. I'm going to take nap. Wake me if there's a crisis." He hesitated briefly over his choice of words. "On second thought, don't bother."

"Wait, wait," Jeff Ray pleaded. "Where the hell am I?"

"I told you kid...2007!" He flashed an impish grin before flopping down on an adjacent couch. "Oh, yeah...you're also in Area 51," he said absently as he closed his eyes.

"He's right, Mr. Peavey," Robert Keen interjected. "I'm afraid you're going to have to come with us right now."

Jeff Ray looked alarmed but Keen reassured him. "It's okay. We just need some information from you. Full name, birthday...just basic stuff."

Briefly weighing his options, he chose discretion as the better part of valour and nodded his assent.

"You are going to have to stay here indefinitely until we can figure out what to do with you, but it's pretty comfortable, for most part. Just ask Lurgo," Keen said. "He's been here since the 50's."

A week later, Jeff Ray Peavey sat glumly in his room at Area 51, which was much nicer than his last apartment, he had to admit. The thought, however, did not cheer him. Keen had dropped by a few days ago to see if he needed anything, and Dr. Melnik had talked to him yesterday, mostly about how he was feeling about being, as he put it, "a man out of time. But the person he really wanted to talk to was still a no show. Lurgo Wix had been conspicuous by his absence since they had returned from the future, and he needed to talk to him. He knew they were connected somehow...he was sure of it. But he had no idea why.

A knock on the door shook him out of his reverie and he beckoned whoever it was to come in. Agent Keen made his way into the room with Dr Melnik, followed by a woman Jeff Ray had never met, and bringing up the rear, the previously absent Lurgo Wix. He smiled ruefully at Jeff Ray, and gave him a finger pistol greeting, another thing he had picked up from those endless B-movies.

"Mr. Peavey, it's a pleasure to meet you. My name is Sarah Wells. I'm the director of the Wix Project. I'm sure you have a lot of questions."

"Actually, I think I'm pretty much up to speed on the situation," he replied. "This is 2007, and I'm in Area 51. I have travelled back in time from your future and my present through a portal created by an intergalactic sock-finder that somehow has the ability to predict the end of the world. It was brought here in 1947 by an alien from some place called Bellaxitor. That about do it?" he asked pointedly.

"Almost," Wells replied. "There is the matter of your being in this timeline, which is why we came to speak to you."

"Because there's a younger version of me out there somewhere, and having two of us in the same timeline could screw things up pretty bad. That's a paradox, right?" he asked.

"Actually, that's what we came to talk to you about. We've done an exhaustive search of birth records and various government data-bases and we can't find any trace of you...at all. It's like you don't exist."

Jeff Ray was nonplussed. "Well, I'm standing right here."

"Indeed, you are," she replied. "It appears the presence of your future self in this timeline has erased your past self from it altogether."

"Well, I guess that takes care of the paradox thing," he said. "So now what? Do I have to stay here the rest of my life like him?" He pointed at Lurgo.

"We'd like you to remain here, for the time being anyway," Wells replied. "But we would hope you'll want to stay of your own accord to work with us on future projects."

Before he could answer, a guard came to the door of the room and beckoned the Director outside. After a moment, she returned.

"Gentlemen, it appears the Sock Finder alarm has gone off again." She looked disapprovingly over at Lurgo.

"Hey, don't look at me," he said innocently. "I swear I haven't touched that thing since we got back."

"Regardless, it looks like we've got another extinction level situation. Agent Keen, meet me in the Level 12 lab."

"I'll need some time to assemble a team," he replied.

"No need, Agent. I think you've got a pretty good group right here." She turned to Peavey and Lurgo. "What do you say, gentlemen? Feel like saving the world again?"

Lurgo looked at Peavey and flashed him the grin that had charmed the pants off the ladies and the money out of countless pockets across the cosmos.

"It could be fun," he smirked.

"Sure...what the hell," Jeff Ray said. "There's nothing on TV in this dump except re-runs anyway. Ya know, you guys should really think about getting Netflix."

"Net-*what*?" Wells asked.

"Never mind," he said.

After the three left the room, Dr Melnik turned to go himself. Before he could leave, Wells called after him.

"Doctor," she said.

"Yes Director?"

"When you get back to the lab, can you and your team do me a small favour?"

"Anything, Ma'am."

"Can you please come up with another name for that device? 'Sock-finder' seems like a pretty innocuous name for something that... important, don't you think?"

"Actually, I think it's kind of cute," he replied cheerfully.

She looked at him thoughtfully. "Perhaps you're right."

He wasn't, of course.

STEVEN FRITZ

 Steven Fritz graduated from the University of Maryland, became a Naval Aviator and flew helicopters and maritime patrol aircraft in the US Navy. After leaving active duty, he earned a Ph. D. in Radiation Biophysics at the University of Kansas. He spent several years as a medical school faculty member before managing a seed stage venture fund and a stint as an avionics entrepreneur. He's been infatuated with science fiction since his youth and has been writing SF full time for three years. His story in this volume is a prequel to his recently completed novel IX New Millennium, set a thousand years after this story on a scarcely imaginable new Earth. Steven also working on a new series set in the asteroid belt and on Mars in a near future. You can follow Steven on his website at InigoPress.com.

IX DEPARTURE

BY STEVEN FRITZ

"Father Ignatius!" The voice seemed to come from everywhere.

I saw myself in a dimly lit, empty room, lying in bed. Visions swirled through my mind, snippets of things I couldn't pin down. My father going off to war - again. He hugged and kissed my mother, then me, tears streaming down our faces. Then he was gone, never to return. I cried and reached for my mother, but she receded from my grasp into a mist.

I stood in a grove of trees, watching a burial party from afar, my mother standing next to an open grave. A flag draped the coffin above it. A priest solemnly intoned, "Now we commit our departed brother Ignatius to the arms of his Savior." The flag had become a black robe, a cassock, hung carelessly over the container of my last mortal remains. I tried to scream.

Someone laid hands on me from behind - no above. The bishop of Baltimore anointed me as I lay prone on the cold marble of an altar in the theology school at Woodstock, Maryland, home of the new American province of the Society of Jesus, ordaining me a priest.

Voices again, far away. "Your cancer is stage 4, Father," the doctor said. "The metastatic disease is in your brain. There's little more we can do. Prayer is all you have left." I was strangely at peace. The pain was just a memory. Everything was just a memory. All my muscles relaxed.

"He's crashing!" someone shouted. "Defib!"

No, I thought. Let me go. But they didn't. My whole body convulsed, and my consciousness catapulted out of my dreams. Everything hurt. I lay in a dimly lit medical procedure room, surrounded by harried people in skimpy clothing. No, not skimpy just lightweight and easy to clean.

Then the pain returned. But this was unfamiliar. My cancer hurt only in my belly. I always felt bloated, even as I shed weight it had taken me a decade to accumulate. Now my whole body felt on fire. But I felt lean, almost skeletal by comparison with my former Falstaffian self. I managed a moment of mirth, somehow, even as I writhed. Falstaff I had definitely never been.

"Core temp is rising steadily," a woman droned. "Heartbeat's stable at 75,"

"I think we have him back," another woman said. An older voice, calmer, definitely in charge.

"Dr. Ghirardi," a male voice said. "Gene scan is done. No cancer."

"At least we have that to be thankful for," the Woman in Charge said.

Dr. Ghirardi. I knew that name. My mother had spent enormous sums on Dr. Ghirardi's research into cryosleep. I sometimes thought my mother planned never to die. This Dr. Ghirardi had long sable hair pulled into a bun, a flawless ivory complexion, hazel eyes a man could get lost in. A surgical mask and cap hid further details. Faint wrinkles around the corners of her eyes suggested she was older than me. I vaguely remembered my mother's Dr. Ghirardi had a son, not a daughter, but he had been a child. This must be his granddaughter.

We exchanged glances. Hers crinkled above her sterile mask. "Welcome back, Father Ignatius. Welcome to the twenty second century." Her demeanor relaxed into competent doctor mode as she turned back to her work. My pain was gone, replaced by a chill that filled my body.

"You can reduce the heat, John," she said to one of the people around me. "Let's see how well he's stabilizing." She returned her attention to me. "You're going to be famous, Father Ignatius. You're the earliest sleeper to be revived and cured by gene therapy. Your cancer is gone. We did it while you slept." She blinked her smile on again, momentarily, then she issued more orders in that quiet, commanding voice.

"Earliest sleeper?" I mumbled.

She returned her attention to me. "We've revived other sleepers successfully, but you've been asleep almost seventy-five years. That's a record by two decades. My grandfather must have done his work well. It was tricky a few times during revival, but your cancer is gone and your brain seems to be working. At least you can speak."

"I don't understand," I said. " The last thing I remember was walking with my mother. I was dying. We walked by her car and two large men jumped out. They injected me with something and bundled me into my mother's car. Then nothing. Until today."

Something came into her eyes, her overall expression hidden by the mask. "Don't you remember being prepped for cryosleep?" Her voice was louder, higher than before.

"No," I replied. "I remember walking, then being stuck with a needle, then shoved into her car, then nothing."

"Damn," she muttered, eyes flashing. Her smile returned. A professional mask. "Your inception must have been involuntary. We're both lucky you're still alive. My grandfather's ethics were, well, malleable. His science was impeccable but keeping it going financially strained him to the breaking point."

She stopped, averted her gaze.

"Apparently beyond the breaking point, "she murmured, as if to herself.

"My mother funded his research," I said. "I remember that. She was quite excited by it." A thought materialized. "Is she asleep like me?"

Her eyes turned downward. It amazed me how expressive just eyes could be.

"Father Ignatius, I'm sorry to tell you, your mother died at home alone. I'm sorry for your loss. My grandfather felt terrible he didn't get to her in time. But she's been dead for decades."

Mother gone? Seventy-five years?

"The blanket's completely off now, Doctor," John said. "His core temp is slightly low but coming up nicely."

"What's going to happen to me?" Even I could hear the neediness in my voice.

"You're going to live," she said. "I know it's disorienting. Once we get you stabilized, we'll have to talk. You'll be fine."

By now the medical team had slackened their frenetic pace. They seemed to be packing up equipment, moving trays of utensils away from my body. A woman next to me disconnected an IV drip from a line in my left arm. The doctor stripped off her mask, revealing a petite nose, a mouth I found barely too wide for her face, a strong chin. She was really quite pretty.

Bob, a fellow novice in the Society of Jesus, had once told me he liked looking at attractive women even though in the revitalized Jesuit order celibacy was strictly enforced. He had said, "Just because I'm not having dinner doesn't mean I can't look at the menu." Apparently Bob was having at least an appetizer, because an irate father from the housing development next door complained to the Novice Master. Bob was gone the next day.

Dr. Ghirardi finished her supervision and turned her attention back to me. "Father, we need to talk soon about your recovery, but I want you to know your cancer is completely cured. Not only are you a record setter in cryosleep longevity, your cancer is the most advanced ever handled by gene therapy."

The fog of dreams had gone. "Why now?" I asked. "Why did you revive me now?"

"Because we could," she said with a wide grin. "We were sure we could cure the cancer. To be honest, I was more concerned that we wouldn't be able to revive you. Also to be honest, there was some tension between the cost of keeping you asleep and the likelihood of reviving you at all."

"If my mother is dead, who decided to awaken me?"

"I did," the doctor said, looking directly at me. "Your mother entrusted decisions about your care to my grandfather in her will. My grandfather transferred the responsibility to my father. My father passed the baton to me. I thought this would be the best time to try. I hope you forgive me."

It was almost an apology, but not quite.

"Forgiveness is my job." I almost meant it.

"We'll talk more after we're finished with you. I'm leaving the team to wrap things up. I have paperwork to do. I'll see you in an hour." With that she walked out of the procedure room, stripping off her gloves as she went.

Dr. Ghirardi visited me in a recovery room shortly after my revival. I was still not able to eat; my nourishment came from an IV bag hanging next to my bed. She wore clean scrubs, a stethoscope dangled around her neck.

"Good morning, Father," she said in a cheery voice. "I know it's actually after noon, but I wanted to congratulate you on the start of your second life. How do you feel?"

"I feel a little weak, but no pain. My cancer is truly gone?"

"Entirely. We've improved your DNA repair genes to prevent a recurrence. You shouldn't have to worry about it again."

"What year is it?" I asked.

"It's 2150, September," she replied. "Have you had a chance to think what you'll do with your new life?"

"I don't know." I had accepted the fact mother was dead. I still wasn't sure how I felt about her kidnapping me. "I was expecting to die. I haven't had a chance to think about living."

"Well, you're going to be famous. Do you want to be famous?"

"Why would I be famous?"

"You were one of my grandfather's earliest successful inceptions into cryosleep and the earliest cancer patient to be cured after revival. The world will be excited."

"I don't want to be famous," I said.

"We don't have to make a major news release while you're still here. Maybe you can find someplace to live before the news breaks."

"I was a Jesuit. I'd like to go back."

"The Jesuits were apparently confused about you," she said. "I talked to the head man, what do you call him, the Provincial? He didn't realize you were still alive. But we explained everything. When you're ready to leave the hospital, if you want to go back, they said we could send you to Wernersville. That's not far from here, just west of Philadelphia."

Wernersville. The house of my dreams. The site of the Novitiate in which I had first become a member of the Society of Jesus - a Jesuit. I loved its wide marble corridors, its dining hall brimming with ideal-istic young men. I especially loved the ornate Crypt Chapel in the basement where Mr. and Mrs. Brady, whose money had built the Novitiate during the twentieth century, in the depth of the Great Depression, were now buried. Walks with other novices in the coun-tryside, by then its bucolic charm being strangled by creeping tendrils of exurbia, had seemed like heaven. I found peace there after my father's untimely death and my mother's suffocating control of my life. At Wernersville I had at last been free. I longed to go home.

Unfortunately Dr. Ghirardi wasn't able to protect me from fame. Someone leaked my story to the news media about a week after she revived me. I awoke to see a mob outside my window, vans and crews and cameras with unfamiliar logos. I had no idea how news worked in the twenty-second century, but the circus on the roundabout in front of the hospital looked familiar.

The street clothing in my room must have been provided by the hospital; none of my own possessions remained. Dr. Ghirardi showed up as I was finishing getting dressed.

"Father Ignatius," she said. "I'm so sorry. I'll fire whoever alerted the media to your revival. But there's still a huge crowd outside. Are you sure you don't want to talk to them?"

I shook my head. "No. Not at all. How can I get out of here?"

"We'll take you out the back door in a hearse," she said with a satisfied smile. "That'll be the last thing these vultures expect."

Sadly, the vultures found out. As the hearse pulled out of the garage into a side street, the mob converged. Reporters and camera people jostled and pushed one another as they fought for a position to photograph me. Since I was in the passenger seat, the scrum of reporters swirled around the right side. Microphones were thrust toward me, despite the closed window, and reporters shouted questions.

"Father Ignatius, how does it feel after being resurrected?"

"Father Ignatius, does the Pope approve of your return?"

"Ignatius, how do you feel about the rumor you're a devil in disguise?"

I turned to Roberto, the driver. He shrugged.

The hearse accelerated away from the hospital, leaving the pedestrians behind. Several vans followed in our wake. I crouched down in the seat, wishing I were invisible. Once we got to Wernersville the gate to the novitiate property opened to admit us. The gate closed, shutting out the reporters in our wake. We were able to drive up the hill to the house of studies without an escort. Roberto stopped in the circular drive in front of the house and I ascended the staircase for the first time in almost a century.

A novice met me at the door.

"Father Ignatius?" he asked in a hesitant voice.

"Yes. Am I expected?"

"The Provincial asked me to take you to your room." His extreme youth made me realize how young I had been when I joined.

"Thank you," I said. "Have you been here long?"

"I got here three weeks ago," he said. "Where is your luggage?"

"I don't have any."

Once we entered the house he stopped talking. The Society had reinstituted silence in the house for novices. He led me to a tiny room with a bed, desk, wardrobe and minuscule bathroom. A wave of his hand invited me in, then he turned and walked away without a sound, leaving me to my thoughts.

With nothing better to do, I left my room and walked down the hall to the exit leading to the roof of the cloister walk, a small rectangular, covered portico enclosing a garden of stones, flowers, and bushes. I pushed the door open and walked into the fragrant autumn air of Pennsylvania.

Smells of leaves and harvested wheat wafted through the cool air. The sun had long since sunk beneath the roof of the main building and the air was cool. From the roof of the cloister walk, I scanned the panorama of the countryside that had enthralled me a century before. The city of Reading had already turned on its lights against the gathering darkness. The lights sparkled faintly against a landscape slowly dissolving into pale greens and blues of twilight. It never failed to amaze me that this humblest of cities had beckoned then with the voice of Sodom and Gomorrah, speaking soft whispers of sin and decadence in the sacred silence of the Novitiate.

"*Father Ignatius, the Novice Master wants to see you,*" the novice at my elbow said in the doggerel Latin of the Novitiate. He hurried away on invisible feet, the hem of his black cassock sweeping the walkway clean as he went back inside. I cast a last lingering glance at the city and followed him.

The Jesuit Provincial, the head of the Province, was making his customary visit with the individual members of this house of the Society in the office of the Master of Novices. The novice either hadn't known how to refer to the Provincial or hadn't even realized he was the Provincial. I knocked on the office door, heard the Provincial's formal "Come", and entered the familiar room.

The Provincial stood at the window with his back to me, staring into the gloom at bands of novices returning from their evening recreation. I could hardly believe here in the century of space travel, artificial intelligence and high bioscience, I found the medieval trappings of the Society of Jesus I had joined as a boy in the age of nuclear war and fossil fuel. When the Society left its medieval ways behind in the last half of the twentieth century, it had been with mixed feelings. The winds that had borne the Society then were different than were blowing today. My own entry into the Society in the mid-twenty-first century had been at the leading edge of the restoration of the old ways.

"Sit down, Father Ignatius," the Provincial said, not unkindly. He continued looking out in silence for an interval which approached uncomfortable length, then turned and sat down behind the ancient desk which Father Tom Gallagher had graced during my years as a Novice.

"Ignatius, you must know you present me with a dilemma. You don'

t know just how much of a dilemma. When Dr. Ghirardi revived you from cryosleep, she called me to discuss your return. We had no idea you were alive. Your kidnapping was one of the most famous unsolved disappearances in Berks County history. Tell me what you remember."

"I discussed this with Dr. Ghirardi," I explained. "My mother had come to the hospice center to take me for a walk. We went to the old churchyard next door. I was exhausted and wanted to go back. Two men injected me with something and bundled me into my mother's car. The next thing I remember is being revived at the Institute."

"How long has it been since you were revived?"

I glanced at my watch for the date. "Less than a month, Father," I replied. "I left the hospital today. Dr. Ghirardi told me I spent seventy-five years in cryosleep."

"How do you find the twenty-second century? Better, I hope, than I do."

"I'm too new to answer that. I was dying, and this century gave me my life back. In my first life, we worried about the obvious effects of the changing climate. If anything has changed, I haven't been here long enough to appreciate it. But none of this technology which my century promised has changed the fact of human suffering. After seeing images of the famine in Bangladesh on the news last night, I was quite unable to eat. Perhaps it's the legacy of the cancer."

"Ignatius," the Provincial said in a troubled voice. "I have to ask something of you and I cannot, in good conscience, insist you obey. You have become a trial to the Society of Jesus since your awakening. I know your mother had you kidnapped and placed in cryosleep against your will. The fact it was done at such great expense, even though the money was hers, is being taken by many as an affront against the vow of poverty. The money lavished on your sleep, revival, and genetic surgery could have supported our charitable works in Mexico for the entire period you were gone."

The Provincial sighed. "To me, Ignatius, the money doesn't matter. I could see that money burned in a bonfire without flinching. Ten times that sum would not have cured poverty in this hemisphere, nor in truth, dented it. The problems are too systemic and deeply embedded. But it does provide an embarrassment to the Society in certain quarters. You cannot know this yet, but there is danger that Rome will suppress the Society again, perhaps within the year. You have provided ammunition for the detractors. This may be neither your fault nor mine, but it is a fact. Do you understand my position?"

"I don't know," I said, knowing all too well. "When I was diagnosed with cancer, I made my peace with God and the idea of dying. Unfortunately, my mother didn't. She turned me over to a doctor who claimed to have solved the problems of putting a person in cryogenic hibernation, then reviving them. My mother funded a lot of his work and believed in him." I smiled, or maybe grimaced. "Apparently she was right. Here I am. But I never asked for this nor agreed to it."

"As I have been informed." He ran his hand through his thinning hair. "Do you know what they're saying in Rome?"

I shook my head.

"They're saying Ignatius Ryan is not alive. They say he died decades ago, and the Devil has returned in his guise to tempt us to doubt our faith in the Resurrection."

"Dear God! Surely, they can't believe that! I am not the only reanimated sleeper."

"From their perspective, that's even more damning. An army of demons led by a dead priest. At the moment, it's just fringe theory. I don't know whether it might be believed by anyone. But I received a letter for you from Rome yesterday. You'd better read it yourself."

He handed me an envelope bearing the Papal coat of arms. It was unsealed. No surprise, the superiors still read the mail. Inside I found a single sheet of stationery. It contained a single paragraph.

To our brother in Christ, Father Ignatius Xavier Ryan, Pax Christi,

It is our painful duty to request of you, my son, to undertake a journey for Mother Church from which there is no return. Sent to us by God from another century, we are compelled to ask you to continue your journey through time to become the first missionary to the future. The fires of Christianity are burning lower and we cannot be certain what will happen. We are resolved to send you, our son, to carry a message of faith, undimmed by ages of waiting, that Jesus will yet return. Go with God.

Humberto Sanchez Garcia Cordoba, John XXV

I looked up, stunned. "What does this mean?"

The Provincial became businesslike. "There is a ship, a time shuttle, to be launched in two weeks. It will be programmed for a deep cometary orbit, returning in eleven hundred years.

"The Pope wants me to go into space?"

"I understand the ship was already programmed to leave then. It's automated. Adding you seems to have been a last-minute change."

"And they expect me to survive a thousand years in an add-on cryosleep system?" My voice rose, I started to hyperventilate.

"I'm assured that cryosleep technology has been improved, and there is little risk. You will return in the year 3260 of the present calendar. A gift to the future." Bitterness laced his voice. "At a cost of one trillion dollars."

"And one life. I won't survive another cryosleep. Please, help me."

As he ran his hand through his hair, I could see it was graying as well. "I might be able to help," he said, "but the help will not be without cost, to both of us."

"Anything."

"I will be burned at the stake before I demand this in the spirit of obedience. But if I simply refuse to demand your obedience, Rome will appoint another who will. As Provincial, I can release you from your vows. But you must leave the Society immediately, tonight. I'll see you will be given a place in the world. But it cannot be here."

"No," I blurted out. My gut churned, I felt faint. "I'm a stranger here in this century. What will I do? How will I live? You can't ask this."

"You'll survive, Ignatius. Dr. Ghirardi told me you're famous. You can sell your story to the media."

"And spend the rest of my life as a circus clown? No. I couldn't bear that."

"Then I cannot save you from going on this journey. I am truly sorry, Ignatius."

"I'll ... I'll go to Rome. I'll speak to His Holiness. Surely I can convince him this is madness."

"You won't," the Provincial said. "His secretary, Cardinal Bienvenista, controls his schedule. I'm sure he's behind all of this. He is an inflexible, implacable man."

"I have to try. "

"Then I wish you luck, Ignatius." He stood, offered his hand. "You can leave for Rome tomorrow. Go with God."

"Father Ignatius."

A monsignor stood before me, immaculate in his red-trimmed cassock. Thin almost to the point of emaciation, with thick black hair, a round face with a faintly bronze complexion and epicanthic folds in the corners of his eyes, the monsignor displayed a haughty mien, a triumphal smile. While I waited in Cardinal Bienvenista's enormous anteroom for over two hours, other supplicants for the Cardinal's favor arrived. The monsignor ushered each immediately into the inner sanctum. I could see the calculated insult but do nothing about it.

"The Cardinal will see you now." he vouchsafed eventually.

He turned and walked away without awaiting a reply. I hurried after him. As I entered the Cardinal's office, its tiny size surprised me. He must keep the huge anteroom for show, a compact office for business. The Cardinal himself seemed short, maybe sixty years old, with a full head of white hair and a jowly, heavily lined face. He sat behind an ornate wooden desk that may have dated to the Middle Ages. He wore a black cassock with red buttons and a red sash tied around his waist. A red skullcap perched on his head. The neutral expression on his face gave nothing away.

"Ignatius Ryan," he said.

"Your Eminence," I began.

"Silence!" He said it quietly, without a hint of expecting anything but obedience. "You have been allowed to visit that I may see you for myself. You have not been invited to speak."

He regarded me fixedly, then scanned up and down my now lean frame. I was grateful I had been given a cassock in the modern Catholic (i.e., medieval) style that fit me. My girth in my prior life had been substantial but the cancer took most of it away, along with everything else. My old cassock would have fit me like a tent.

"So," he said at last. "You may speak."

"Eminence, I was given a message from His Holiness, the Pope, asking me to undertake a journey... "I wasn't sure what to say next.

"Directing." he said, his voice so low as to be barely audible but his diction clipped and precise.

"I beg your pardon?"

"The Holy Father was directing you to undertake the journey, not asking you to."

"Your pardon. Directing me to undertake a journey. But I was hoping this trial might pass me by. I underwent cryosleep against my will. The methods they used were untested. My cancer was cured by this century's treatments, but I nearly died. I fear I will not survive another period of it."

The Cardinal's eyes narrowed. "Do you fear death, Father?" he asked.

"If death were not to be feared," I countered, almost whispering, "the Resurrection would have no meaning."

His features set in a mask of disdain. "But in light of the Resurrection you should have no fear of death." His voice became brusque. "No, I do not believe you fear death. What you fear, I believe, is that you will not be allowed to pollute the Church with your presence in this century."

"Pollute?" I managed to say. "I don't understand."

"There are those who believe you're a demon assuming the identity of a priest who did not have the courage of his vocation seventy-five years ago," he said, as if that implied he was not one of them. "That you're here to try to undermine the teaching of the Church with the undisciplined ideas of an earlier, discredited century."

"You can't believe that!"

"I might believe some or all of it," he said with a touch of cynicism in his tone. "Or I might not. But whether I believe it is unimportant. The horns of the dilemma are these. Either you are who you say you are and would be willing to obey the will of the Holy Father, or you are in fact a malign spirit, whether natural or supernatural, who means to do the Church harm. But you must be part of the clergy to have maximum impact. If you're truly Father Ignatius Ryan, you will obey the Holy Father even against your will. If you're not who you seem to be, you must still obey, or lose your status within the Church. Either way, you can do no harm."

"I don't want to do harm," I said. "But I can't believe the Holy Father wishes me to go on a journey to my death."

The Cardinal half smiled, as if at a private joke. "Surely you're not calling me a liar?"

"No," I blurted. "But there may be a misunderstanding. I need to know."

The Cardinal's smile broadened. "I think you'll find the Pope is an otherworldly man. But I can afford to humor you. Monsignor Chang, take Father Ignatius to the Pope. I don't want him to misunderstand."

Monsignor Chang returned the Cardinal's smile and gestured toward the door. "This way, Father."

———

Chang left me in the corridor outside the Pope's personal office while he went in. He returned minutes later.

"His Holiness will see you now," he said with an unpleasant grin.

The door still stood open and I entered at Chang's direction. In a room even tinier than the Cardinal's office, the Pope sat at a small desk and waved me into a chair.

"My son," the Pope said. "I read about your revival. Monsignor Chang tells me you're troubled."

"Holy Father," I said. "Cardinal Bienvenista wants me to go back into cryohibernation. The cryosleep chamber is aboard a spaceship that's going to leave Earth for a thousand years. The Cardinal says you are ordering me to go on this journey. Is that your wish?"

"Ignatius, have you prayed over this journey?" the Pope asked in a soft, gentle voice.

"I ... I've been recovering from the hibernation and the cancer treatment. I've found it difficult to pray."

"I have prayed about it. Tell me, do you think the Church will survive this time of trouble? Few believe strongly in anything anymore."

"The Church has survived persecutions before. I hope for the future."

"As do I," the Pope said, looking beyond me into infinity. "But I have a strong feeling it may not. I cannot say God has spoken to me, but I have had recurring visions of the world dissolving in fire and ice. I feel called to send you on this journey. I am responsible for the people of God and I need this from you. Please, will you go?"

"I don't know if I can, Holy Father," I said. "I have a feeling I won't survive."

"Ignatius, I leave it in your hands and God's. I know you will make the right choice."

It wasn't what I wanted, but it was a choice. "I'll try to do the right thing. May I have your blessing?"

"Of course," he said, sliding from his chair to kneel on the wooden floor. I did likewise. He took a small crucifix from his cassock and placed it in my hands. Then he wrapped his own hands around mine. He began murmuring in Latin. I couldn't concentrate on his meaning, but I felt a sense of peace radiating from him.

When he finished, he put the crucifix back in his robe, stood and embraced me.

"Go with God, my son," he said.

I left with Chang, having no idea what I was going to do.

When we reached the Cardinal's office, Chang took me right in. The theater of humiliation had already played out.

"Did you see the Pope?" the Cardinal asked.

"I did."

"And?"

"He told me he trusted me to make the right decision."

"Your choice is simple. Remain a priest and go on this journey or leave the church forever. You can earn a living as a trained monkey dancing to the tune of the media - and others even worse."

"Worse?"

"I believe the Provincial shared the rumor about being a demon in disguise?"

"You can't take that seriously!"

"There are those who would worship you. Does that tempt you?"

"No!"

"Then it would seem your choice is made."

"Please," I began.

"Enough, you have chosen." He turned to the monsignor. "Monsignor Chang, you will escort Father Ignatius to the Vatican hospital where preparations for cryosleep will be undertaken." He turned back to me. "Your ship awaits in orbit."

Finally, the Cardinal smiled, like a hungry tiger. "I will assume you are a loyal son of the Church. You will have an opportunity given to no one else. You will be sent forward in time a millennium. To ensure the message of Christ survives, you will have copies of the Scripture in ten languages. You're our gift to the future. Thus may you repay your cowardice in the face of death. Go with God, Father Ignatius." He waved his hand vaguely as if in blessing and turned his attention elsewhere. The monsignor smiled a predatory smile and led me away to my fate.

Once outside in St. Peter's square, Chang joined me in a taxi to my hotel, where I collected my few things to take to the hospital. He watched me like a hawk, but I scarcely noticed him. My fate was sealed, I felt I was facing death once again.

Why? The hierarchy of the church seemed to have precious little compassion for me. They had offered me a choice that was no choice at all. The Pope seemed a kindly man, but the Cardinal had made the final decision. I had faced death from cancer with a measure of peace, but then I had seen it as an unavoidable act of God. Now it was the vengeful act of a man who should have done better. My mind was in turmoil as the taxi arrived at the Vatican hospital. Chang escorted me inside the hospital and accompanied me to a special suite for preparations.

The hospital preparation took five days. The day after this was complete, I was flown to Kenya where I would board the launch vehicle to take me to a pan-European space station in low orbit. Monsignor Chang ushered me personally to the launch site, taking no chance I might escape my fate. What few personal possessions I had Chang carried in a small case.

I was in a semi-catatonic stupor most of this time. When I thought of cryosleep I desperately wanted escape. When I thought of escape, I wanted the Church to enfold me. I tried to pray but words elude me.

The launch into orbit was anticlimactic. I was taken to the satellite, passed to the control of an administrator who took me to meet the pilot who would take me to the ship. He was about twenty-five, blond and muscular, with an open face and friendly manner. He helped me into a pressure suit, then donned his own. We passed through an airlock to space. I was numb, handled more like a piece of cargo than a passenger.

"Father Ignatius!"

The pilot's words pulled me out of my reverie. I saw around me an EVA shuttle taking me from the space station to the ship that was to be my prison. The shuttle itself was an open framework with engines at both ends and a space in the middle for cargo and crew. It felt like I was inside the skeleton of a tiny building without walls.

The shuttle pilot floated in front of me, upside down with respect to my orientation. It was all I could do to keep nausea at bay. I focused on the outside universe, stars without number against a black background. It seemed to help.

The pilot flipped upright, at least with respect to me. "Father, you were somewhere else mentally. I called your name several times. Are you feeling well?"

I swallowed, managed to settle my stomach somewhat, tried to smile. "I'm not used to weightlessness. Or being in a pressure suit. It's too tight. I'm not normally claustrophobic but this is strange."

The pilot waved a hand. "It happens to all of us at some point. My first orbital trip I couldn't keep anything down. I had to cut the mission short. But I got used to it."

"Where are we?" I asked.

He consulted a data tablet clipped to one of the bars that made up the open frame of the vehicle. "We're approaching your ship." His voice held traces of my own original Midwestern accent. "Do you understand what needs to happen when we arrive?"

"No."

He hesitated. "The first thing you need to do is get into a one-piece body suit to help maintain temperature control during the hibernation process. After that, I start a venous line for the drugs. When I get you settled, we start with a light sedative."

"Settled?" I asked.

"You'll be in a simple cryosleep container, sort of like a bed with sides."

"A coffin."

"Not really."

"Listen," I said haltingly. "You seem to be recalling this from memory, not experience. Do you know what you're doing?"

My anxiety must have seemed palpable. He smiled. "I'm a revival tech, I don't often do inceptions. But the training is the same and revival is a lot more complex. Inception is much easier than revival. So yes, I know what I'm doing."

He cleared his throat and continued. "Next I'll insert a dual flow line for your venous blood. At first, it'll chill your body lightly. You'll feel somewhat cool, but the sedative will take the edge off. I understand you were unconscious when they did your first hibernation, is that right?"

"I must have been. I don't remember a thing."

"That's not good idea. In fact, when you were first put into hibernation it was a miracle they didn't kill you. We prefer our subjects conscious, so we can monitor their state of mind – and they can tell us if anything seems to be going wrong."

"Well," I sighed. "I was dying anyway."

"Not this time. Which is a very good thing. You can only imagine how hard a good inception is when the patient is sick or wounded."

I was surprised. "Wounded?"

"Yeah. I've done revivals on guys who were missing limbs, gut shot, massive head injuries. It usually doesn't go well. Either one, inception or revival. But this will be easy, you're in great shape. I can handle this, no problem."

There was a muted sound and our vehicle gently touched the capsule. I was taken by surprise, as I hadn't seen a capsule approaching at all. Even a closer look failed to convince me of what I was seeing. It was matte black in color, mainly visible because there were no stars in a roughly ovoid, featureless space about twice the size of a large city bus. Its surface was a collection of randomly oriented flat surfaces with remarkably smooth joins. It reflected absolutely nothing. I had no idea how we were supposed to get in.

"Cool, huh?" he asked. "I pinged it for entry. One of the surfaces will open in a minute and we can go in."

"I don't want to go," I told him.

"Father Ignatius, I don't want to make you go. But if I bring you back, they'll just have someone else bring you here. The way the political situation is going, you're probably going to be better off away from Earth anyway."

No sooner had he spoken than a patch of surface irised open to allow us admittance and light spilled out from inside. The tech/pilot grabbed a bag and entered. He turned to me and I could see his face, expectant, waiting for me to come inside. I acquiesced, as I always did.

The opening closed behind me as I floated through. The universe outside vanished. Inside, though, the interior was brightly lit. I saw a room with a table and two doors. One door led to a somewhat smaller room containing what looked like a transparent box about the size of a coffin. A thick, soft lower surface floated on a liquid layer, a top lay against the wall next to it. Beside the doorway there was a flat working surface where the pilot secured his bag with a Velcro strap.

"Time to do this, Father," he said.

———

I stripped. The air was reasonably warm but not hot. The pilot handed me a one-piece jumpsuit, which I donned. At his direction I climbed into the box and used two soft straps to secure myself to its comfortably padded bottom surface. I tried to relax into it, not to think of it as my coffin. He started an IV line in my left arm and injected something, presumably a sedative. Since the box was transparent, I didn't feel claustrophobic, in fact I didn't feel much of anything. It must have been the sedative. He started another line on my right arm with a drip attached.

"Okay so far, Father?" His voice seemed to be coming to me from the end of a tunnel.

"Okay," I managed.

"You will probably be sleepy but try not to actually go to sleep. Are you feeling cold at this point?"

"Not especially."

"Any strange feelings or hallucinations?"

"No."

"Good." He started another line in my left arm, a dual line with a complex valve and two tubes attached to an apparatus about the size of a briefcase. He pressed a button and something, perhaps a pump, began to whir. At first, I didn't feel anything else. Then I began to feel a bit cold and a sluggish.

"I'm feeling cold ... and a bit sleepy."

"That's good Father," he said. "You will probably drift off to sleep in a bit. Most revivals tell me they don't dream, but some do. When they dream, the dreams mostly don't seem to make much sense."

Consciousness seemed evanescent, coming and going as the tech talked to me. "Godspeed, Father," he said. "Pray for me."

It's the last thing I remember of old Earth.

N L SWEENEY

Born in Federal Way, Washington, N. L. Sweeney is a writer of queer, feminist speculative fiction and a current MFA candidate in the University of Washington Bothell's Creative Writing and Poetics program. They have been writing stories since they were old enough to spell (badly). Some of their works have appeared in Twisted, Jeopardy, Flash Fiction Online, and Clamor. When not writing, they keep busy with escaping into video games, brewing cups of tea, and asking if they can pet strangers' dogs.

MOORING LINE

BY N. L. SWEENEY

The rope lay in a languid coil like a boa warming its stomach on a hot granite rock. It lunged then rippled as Lyza pulled it across the living room floor. She wound it over her chest, under her arm, across her back, under the other arm, in a cycle that tightened and tightened. Tucking the end away at her side, she massaged the skin beneath the rough rope.

"I can carry it today, if you want," Jeremy said.

Lyza jumped at the sound of his light but sharp voice. Two weeks still wasn't long enough to get used to company again. She glanced over her shoulder. "You should have told me you were awake."

The boy looked small in his sleeping bag, though his arms had the gangly awkwardness of a teenager. His unevenly shorn brown hair, which he had insisted he would cut with his own knife, hung over his pillow. He lay on his side in the middle of what had once been a living room, his head rested on one of the clumps of fabric that had been stripped from the carcass of the couch. One of the end tables leaned over where it was missing a leg. A few stray pages rent from their protective covers lay scattered over the couch frames, and fragments of amber beer bottles huddled together behind the broken end table. On one of the walls, someone had spray painted in loud scarlet paint "Daniel 7:23". Lyza had never been religious.

She'd slept by the door last night. Smarter to put Jeremy between her and anyone who came seeking the same shelter they sought, but she'd taken the spot instead.

"I wanted to see what you'd do," he said.

"Well say something next time. It's creepy." Lyza rolled up the bedroll with practiced efficiency, lashed it together, and tossed the strap over her shoulder.

Jeremy crawled out of his sleeping bag. "Well?" He held out his hand to offer.

Lyza checked her belt loop and the bags that hung from it. Hunting knife, can-opener, lighter, three matches, box-cutter, Mars Bar, Glock, one cartridge, screwdriver, half-empty canteen.

Jeremy continued, though her back was to him. "Fine, whatever." He shook his head. "Why do you have it anyway. You've never used it." His small hands slipped over the nylon shell of his sleeping roll.

"Tuck before you fold," Lyza said.

More nylon rustling over nylon. "It's not like it looks good on you, either."

She sighed. "It's important." Jeremy opened his mouth, but she cut him off. "If you don't want to walk out of this house alone, you'll let the subject go."

The scowl evaporated from his face. His eyes widened, and he focused back on his sleeping bag.

Lyza laced up the boots she'd taken from a closet upstairs. They pinched her toes, but were an improvement from her last pair, which were more scraps than leather, anyway. Jeremy didn't look up at her when she spoke. "I'll check the kitchen again. We'll leave when I'm back and no later."

The kitchen was worse than the rest of the house. Not because it was dirty. It was clean to the point of sterility. Like finding a flower growing from a patch of Astroturf. Empty spice containers refracted the morning light onto their silver spiraling rack. A full bar of vanilla soap rested on a clear pedestal beside the gleaming sink faucet, like an altar to the god of hygiene.

She almost clasped her hands together and bowed like she'd seen priests do. Almost laughed. Lyza snatched the soap and shoved it into her pocket, leaving the soap dish behind. The cupboards gaped empty as expected. They'd been lucky to find anything the day before. As Lyza looked, she found a can of corn and a one of green beans behind the boards of the cabinet, in a spot you could only feel, not see. Prying open the green beans, she gulped down a handful and walked back into the living room.

She handed Jeremy the rest of the can. He leaned back against one of the ravaged couches.

Lyza didn't let herself imagine a mother sitting with her daughter on the couch. She didn't let herself think about the cool light emanating from the cleaner patch of wall where the TV must have hung. She didn't let herself feel the warm weight of a child's head on her lap.

Lyza tugged at the rope. "Ready?"

Jeremy kept his gaze down, but that did nothing to hide his puffy red eyes. He nodded.

"We can't be out there long," Lyza said.

The boy rolled his eyes. "I know."

She pulled her scarf up over her mouth and pushed open the door. Mist swirled around her, wafting in pools at her feet. She took one last breath of stuffy air before stepping out the door.

The Mist clung to Lyza's clothes and hung in her hair. It wasn't the cold fog that frosted fingertips or curled around mountains. It was like nothing, caught somewhere between the smell of clean paper and flour. The Mist felt dry and empty on her skin, how Lyza imagined desert air felt but without the oppressive heat, yet it was thick, moving like a liquid around her. It filled the empty space, occluding her vision with tufts of cloud. Lyza kept her scarf over her mouth, so the Mist wouldn't rush into her lungs, though she was certain it didn't make a difference. It would take you no matter what you did.

She kept breathing. Kept walking.

The only direction out here was forward. The sound of her footsteps came as percussive sighs. She listened for Jeremy's muffled steps behind her. The ground disappeared in white, and each step became a test of fate. With every footfall, she expected to tumble forward and fall down deeper into furls of fog. Lyza focused on the scratch of the thick cord on her clavicle, on her shoulders. She'd made the loops tighter today. Perhaps too tight. Her toes ached in her new boots, but the leather would flex or her toes would bend.

The landmarks came less frequently. There was no real order to what stayed and what faded into the Mist. Three days ago, they'd passed by a lonely tree, the first Lyza had seen in months. All of its leaves had been stripped off, leaving the gray brown trunk stark and naked.

For whatever reason, the Mist left houses, at least for a little while. But there seemed to be less of those around lately, too. As for people… they didn't last long in the Mist. Lyza looked back where the last house might have been. Even if she could find it again, they needed more food and water. Lyza pulled her scarf away from her lips and let a few drops of tepid aluminum-tasting water fall on her tongue.

She strained her ears for the sound of Jeremy behind her. Usually he talked more while they walked. Even if it was complaints, she appreciated having something to listen to besides her own thoughts. His footsteps sounded as flat and muffled as hers, but his steps came a little quicker. Lyza thought she saw a darker patch of Mist where he might be walking, but it wouldn't have been the first time she saw things. "You there, kid?" she asked.

His voice came back to her like it was farther away than made sense, or like someone had turned down the volume on her ears. "Yeah. Not really anywhere else to go."

She imagined him with his teeth clenched.

Silence and empty footfalls.

A curl of cold guilt twisted in her stomach. "About what I said earlier, I shouldn't have threatened to leave you."

"Everybody leaves," he muttered, just loud enough for her to hear.

Lyza adjusted the rope on her shoulder. "One day. Yes. I won't leave if I can help it."

It didn't help, but the boy had been through too much for empty promises to work. She took another step and her foot sunk where it should have met earth.

This was it, she thought. *Now the fall.* Instead, she just heard a little plop, and she pulled her foot back out of water.

Lyza smiled, which made her cracked lips split. "Jeremy, come here."

Jeremy emerged from the Mist. Lyza slipped the refilled canteen into her pocket and sipped a handful of the cold, silty water, splashing some of it on her face. Jeremy bent down beside her and dunked his entire head. The dirt and grime of not showering for who-knew-how-long made his face look all smudged. His light brown hair hung forward.

His lips twitched up. "What?"

"You look like a drowned weasel," Lyza said.

Jeremy tossed back his hair, glowering, but with a slight air of humor. "Like you look any better, old bat."

"Old?" she demanded. She pretended to be affronted and scooped up some water and splashed him. The genuine widening of his brown eyes made Lyza laugh in spite of herself.

"Hey!" Jeremy spat, but Lyza was already up and moving away when he cupped a handful of water and flung it at her. A few droplets wet her leg.

His laughter rolled out. As the giggles, too, were pulled into the silence around them, he fell onto his back, folding his hands behind his head. "You would have liked Ann."

Lyza sat down and waited for him to continue.

"She always tried looking serious like you, trying to be mom all the time," he said. "She was a lot younger, though." Lyza gave him a half-hearted push and he chuckled. "She used to make up the best stories. Even after it all. She used to tell me stories about penguins learning to fly or about how clowns found their noses. Stories like that. Happy stories. Even when Dad took off, she never forgot how to laugh." He shook his head. His face had softened. Jeremy looked almost tender, innocent, the way a kid was supposed to look.

Lyza pushed the rising lump in her throat away. She knew how this ended. The stories were all the same. She fought the urge to reach out to him, to put his head on her chest, to tell him he was a good boy. But he wasn't hers.

Jeremy's voice lurched then evened out into a monotone drawl. "But, you know." He cleared his throat. "One day, it took her. We'd been staying at these abandoned fairgrounds for a while. I lost her in the fog. And like that she was gone." He brought his fingers up to snap, but the sound came as if it from underwater. His face evened into a flat mask, his lips tightening to a line. "And one day I'll lose you too."

Out on the water, the Mist pulled back, like an invisible cushion nestled between the two. A lake, Lyza guessed, something deep and dark. The surface smoothed to black glass. No wind breathed over the surface. No boats skimmed across the horizon. No pale faces disappeared into the Mist.

She tore her gaze from the water and closed her mind to the thoughts. Jeremy lay on his back, his arm slung over his face to cover his eyes. His skin looked wan. The brown jacket he wore seemed drained of color, like a shirt left out too long in the sun. She'd seen this before. How long had they been sitting here? Lyza stood up, trying to force the tremor from her voice. "Jeremy, we need to go."

Jeremy shook his head. "Why?" And then he laughed. "What's the point?"

Lyza grabbed his arm and pulled.

He wriggled his arm free. "Let go of me!"

"We have to find shelter." She looked around, but all she could see was white and the lake.

"Why? So I can watch you go too?"

"I'm not going anywhere," she said, as much for herself as for him. "Look." She started unwinding the rope, coil by coil until she had about 7 to 8 feet. She tossed the end into his lap. "Wrap it around you. That way you won't lose me in the fog. I'll be right there beside you."

"You will?"

"Yes!" she said harshly. Then again, softer. "Yes, Jeremy. Come on. We have to get you out of this."

Jeremy looked down at himself, turning his whitening hands over in front of him, and stood up. He tied the rope around his waist.

"Is it tight?" Lyza asked. He tugged and it stayed. "Good." Lyza motioned for him to follow, and they left the lake behind.

There had to be a place close. Someplace. Anyplace. Lyza tried not to start running. She couldn't risk either of them falling. Jeremy was too small to carry her, and she hadn't eaten enough the last few days to carry both of them very far. She found herself taking two quick steps then slowing, and then speeding up again. Jeremy kept pace behind her.

His voice sounded hoarse when he spoke, whether from the pace or the Mist, Lyza couldn't tell. "Why are you doing this?" he asked.

The question almost made her stop, but she couldn't. Her feet felt numb and her sense had gone from her fingers. She knew what that meant but didn't want to look down to make sure. "You're my only company."

He sounded disappointed. "Is that all?"

Why these questions at a time like this? Lyza looked above her, behind her, to the side, in the sky, and saw nothing but white. Why *had* she taken him? She'd left the preacher behind while he slept, had to threaten one woman with her knife to make her leave. "You reminded me of someone, I guess."

It wasn't just the muting of the air. His voice was weaker. "Did you have a brother?"

Lyza shook her head even though she knew he wouldn't be able to see it. "I had a daughter."

She mouthed her name. Helena. And with it came the image of her tugging at the oars, sailing away as the clouds swallowed her. Lyza should have been the one in the boat. Not Helena.

Behind her, the rope tugged, and she heard Jeremy stumble. She followed the rope back to him. He wobbled to his feet.

"I'm fine," he insisted. His breath came out in short rasps. His eyes were like polished marble with flecks of brown, and his skin seemed to shine. The fabric of his jacket and jeans looked like the holes made from drops of water on a watercolor painting. Jeremy took another step and waved her on. She moved ahead.

"Lyza," he called from behind her. "Will you tell me a story?"

Lyza gazed ahead. "A story?

"Yeah," Jeremy said. His footsteps came unevenly, tugging at the rope like a fish at the end of its strength. Lyza had to slow her pace. "One about a weasel and a rope." And he gave what must have been meant as a laugh but sounded closer to punctuated breathing.

Lyza had never been good at stories. That had been Roger's thing. If it would keep him going, she had to try. "Once upon a time, there was a small weasel who loved to swim. And every day, he would swim and swim and swim. Once or twice, people even mistook him for an otter." Lyza floundered.

"What–" he stumbled. "What about the rope?"

"Right," she said. "The rope was a poor tool. She always stood in the shed, hanging all alone while the rest of the tools went out to do their jobs. They called her useless so much that eventually, she started calling herself that.

"One day a great rain came pouring down while the weasel was out swimming, and the waters turned choppy. They started swirling and swirling until they made a great whirlpool and caught the poor weasel." Lyza swallowed. It was like her lungs couldn't take in enough air.

"The tools were asked to save him, but the hammer could only hit nails. The screwdriver was only good if there were screws. So they all turned to the rope, and the rope had an idea." Lyza took a deep breath. "She lashed herself to the nearest tree and swung out over the water." Breathe. "The whirlpool tugged at her, but she held on strong and pulled the weasel to safety. And they all lived happily–"

A sharp tug on her waist. Lyza lost her air. The rope fell slack. The Mist seemed to silence even the heavy thump of her heart, but she felt it beating against her rib cage. "Jeremy?" Once more, "Jeremy?" She tugged at the rope, and it whipped toward her. An empty loop wilted in her hands.

She stumbled through the Mist where he should have been, her hands grasping empty air. She called his name again. Nothing. She pulled her scarf away from her mouth and yelled, but the Mist ate up the words. The numbness traveled up her legs and reached her abdomen. The rope's defiant brown seemed to be the only patch of color left.

Her foot carried her, wobbling. Two steps and she hit something hard and thick and solid. A door. Maybe he'd made it inside. Her hand grasped a latch. She threw the door open and fell through the entrance.

The inside was dark, the only light filtering in from a crack in the shutters and a hole in the roof. Stray hay littered the otherwise empty ground. Her breath came easier, but her lungs ached as she fought to pull air. "Jeremy?" she asked once more. Her voice filled the shed.

Lyza leaned herself against a support beam, and the tears came. They seized her, made her fall forward like an animal and scream, and beat her fists on the ground. Blossoms of red bloomed on the floor as she slammed down her hands again and again. She screamed for Jeremy and for Helena as she pushed out to sea. Lyza called for her daughter to come back, tugged and tugged at the mooring line until her daughter finally cut it loose and it hung limp in her grasp. She yelled at herself and at whatever gods could hear.

Clarity came in the form of two images: a high beam and the coil of rope clenched in her fist. She found a stool in one of the stalls and wobbled onto it. Throwing the rope up, she looped it over the thick beam and tightened. Once more. Again. One swift tilt and jolt and one fatal snap was all it would take. Quick. Simple. Her hands gripped the thick braids of the rope until they quivered. She let out her breath, stepped off the stool, and wound the rope once more over her chest, under her arm, across her back. She spun it tight around her.

"No," she whispered. "Not yet."

SHARON KAE REAMER

Now a full-time writer, Sharon Kae Reamer's speculative fiction is inspired by her participation in various archeoseismology projects during her twenty-something years as a senior scientist at the University of Cologne. Locations that include the Praetorium and medieval Jewish settlement in Cologne, ancient Tiryns in Greece, and Greek ruins in Selinunte, Sicily, provide perfect backdrops for creating fantasy stories rich with history and mythology, such as her *Immortal Guardian* and *Schattenreich* novelette series and her five-book *Schattenreich* novel series.

Her love for mixing and mashing science fiction and fantasy continues unabated.

And, of course, she has cats.

More details available at www.sharonreamer.com.

SORBET JUNCTION

By SHARON KAE REAMER

Eldon Bakker paused just inside the entrance to the room containing the organic crystal matrix. He looked around, his shoulder twitching. Even though the white-tiled hallway was dark and deserted, the walls glowed ominously. There was no reason for anyone to be here now. There was no reason for Eldon to be here now either.

He wore his white lab coat, a subterfuge that wouldn't fool anyone, over stretchy functional mountaineering pants that had cost him a month's salary. Alone in his room, waiting for midnight had been pure torture, he shivered and grew stiff with fright.

Eldon took a deep breath stepping in; the thick gray door closed behind him with a soft whoompf. The lights in the raised observation cubicle protruding into the room were out. Abandoned. The last time he'd been in the cubicle he'd been *Prentice* Eldon. He breathed deeply again and adjusted the night vision goggles he'd 'borrowed' from Alice. They hadn't been close friends, but he regretted making yet another enemy. The note he'd left her on top of her gadget box would ensure that she'd never forgive him. The goggles sucked at the skin around his eyes and made everything glow ominously. It was better than groping around in the dark. Or using a flashlight. He'd stuck a tiny one in his pack just before leaving his room, but wanted to have his hands free.

Eldon was drawn to the plastic cylinder, thin but hard, extending from floor to ceiling. No opening anywhere. Within the cylinder was the organic crystal matrix. Together they occupied a good third of the room and made the remaining white walls and a smooth floor of semi-transparent plastic confining. That alone should have sent Eldon running and screaming.

What made him stay was the vision before him. He never thought a doorway to another universe could be so beautiful. If that's really what it was.

Eldon doubted he'd ever see anything so captivating again.

He took a few steps farther in. The leather of his sandals squeaked. He hoped they would be the right shoes. Eldon had a problem with shoes. No matter which ones he wore, they were always the wrong ones. Too formal or too ugly or too new. But these sandals were comfortable and didn't give him blisters. He'd tested them on a few hikes through the bowels of the institute over the last week to make sure.

He didn't test if they were good for running. Eldon was not a model of physical perfection. Too many late nights in the library and too little exercise. He really hoped he didn't have to run.

A pang of doubt gripped his insides. He swayed on his feet. What had possessed him, made him disobey every instruction he'd received since he'd been accepted into the trans dimensional project? He'd learned rebellion early enough and had never unlearned it. Eldon swallowed hard. Now was not the time for recriminations. Or doubt, especially not that. Anger still lurked deep down, but he shoved it away. It would only make him make mistakes. That was the one thing he couldn't afford.

After decontamination, the matrix had been sealed off from everyone. The only contact with the contents of this room since initiation of the crystal growth had been through the bulbous observation cubicle. With his intrusion, Eldon had now violated the pristine environment. Initially, they considered putting everything into vacuum, but Eldon convinced them it might be detrimental to the matrix. They listened to him back then.

There was no odor of antiseptic, no hint of plastic. Eldon longed to smell the crystal matrix. Would it even have a scent? He shrugged off his pack and laid it gently on the floor. Eldon pressed his palm to the smooth plastic of the cylinder, the only barrier between him and his goal. It felt neither warm nor cold, emitted no sound.

He felt transfixed, almost as if he didn't want to go forward. It wasn't too late. He could just walk out the door and go back to his warm bed. No one would ever know.

But anger kept him there. He swayed forward, marveling at how much the crystal structure resembled a living thing, a plant. The glassy blooms had a creamy color and looked as if they had been frosted. They reminded him of lemon sorbet and made him swallow with the memory of that clean, fresh taste. There was only one way to get inside and he dreaded the deed, but could no longer resist trying.

The entire construct was not even advanced enough to be considered beta. Not yet ready for testing, even with inanimate objects, the danger of causing damage to the delicate structure was too great to risk it.

For everyone else, that is.

And what would happen? Would he travel, enfolded in the construct's crystal embrace? The matrix was designed to simulate the circulation and reproduction system of flowering plants. The early discussions, before they'd kicked him out, had centered around which part was operative.

But he knew. Intuition grown from of years of learning to trust himself. It was the blooms. Not the seedpods as the other members of the project had hypothesized. Eldon was convinced that the only way to travel was through the blooms.

The result of his going in: Completely unpredictable. Possibly fatal. Right.

That same bone-deep intuition said this thing was not transdimensional. How could it be? If the universe transcended the four known dimensions, then there must be a way to access them. But no evidence supported the existence of extra dimensions or any cracks in between the known ones. None whatsoever.

Something, someone, held back vital information about what this project was all about. Eldon asked about it. Shortly afterwards, he'd been kicked off.

No, there would be no turning back. His actions were reckless, foolish, reprehensible. But his expulsion from the transdimensional team four weeks ago had started him brooding and planning his revenge. Abruptly cut off from the only thing that mattered to him in many years of his relatively short life, his transcendence from the hellish confinement of his past, he had felt a devastation that threatened to swallow him whole.

He coped the only way he knew how, with his best and first weapon, his imagination. The dream that haunted him mashed together frustration and disbelief, playing out what it would be like to be the first traveler through the bloom. And then the idea had begun to dominate his every waking moment.

His being banned from the project had ostensibly been an anonymous accusation that he was psychologically unfit for his job. He was sure Jady had been behind it. After an initial sappy phase complete with moon-eyed looks and hand-holding, Eldon confided in her about his past one night when they were alone in the library. She'd listened without laughter or pity.

And then they talked about the project, and he confessed to her his doubts about its real purpose. She was not part of the project, and Eldon hoped by discussing things with her, he would gain insight into why his instincts were poking him that something was amiss.

Just after that, Jady changed. Literally overnight. She hounded him relentlessly to get her into the transdimensional project. He told her he had no power over who was included; he was just a Prentice. But she didn't let up.

When he finally broke it off with her – his wanting to be honorable about it had been a big big mistake – she'd been angry. That was to be expected. But Jady turned icy. He heard from others about the increasing frequency of her disparaging remarks There was high statistical probability she'd been free with her insults about Eldon to Master

Arnaud as well. But whatever it was she told the Master had not only gotten her involved with the project. It netted her *instant* promotion to *Prentice* Jady.

To quell the rumors Jady spread about his inadequacy, Eldon volunteered to take a psych test. His confessions to Jady were the only time he'd ever confided in anyone about a past he mostly wanted to forget. And now he deeply regretted doing so.

He failed the test.

They wouldn't tell him why. Maybe he really was unfit. For a few days, he seethed, wondering what was wrong with him. He had a great fear of being alone or confined because of his past, it was true. He'd been broken. They'd stolen every dream he'd ever had. But here, in the Institute of Applied Biomathematics, the IABM, he was never alone and his past had never interfered with his work or with his interactions with others. He'd learned to fix himself.

But all that didn't matter now.

Staring at the white blooms, the seething mass of evolving crystallization not visible to the naked eye, Eldon chuckled in his best mad scientist voice and wondered if he'd ever eat lemon sorbet again. He pulled the diamond-tipped borer from his pack, the metal of the drill cold and reassuring in his hand. There was a note for Malte in the machine shop about that, too.

Eldon took a deep breath and then placed the drill against the plastic cylinder. The drill whined as it bit through the plastic and made him wince. He began to sweat – not from the exertion – but from the fear that ran through his body, more powerful than blood.

What would they do to him? Was there a hole deep and dark enough for the righteousness of his imprisonment where they would drop him? He'd never see the light of day again, let alone taste lemon sorbet. The drill slipped down. He shook his head and stopped to regain his wits, his breath coming in short, sharp pants.

Always before, he'd seen the crystal flower from above and at several removes from where he now stood.

Its beauty was not only the shine of light reflected from its myriad perfect surfaces, but also its intricacy. The seven-point leaves arrayed around the stem *glowed*, a deep vibrant green. The elongated sage green seedpods looked fuzzy, although Eldon knew it was an illusion. Each pod with thousands of tiny hairs sticking out was a single-rowed lattice of crystals.

The white blooms, however, were the most exquisite; sheets of silicon embedded in a growth matrix, interleaved up the bloom's length.

The wonder succeeded in chasing away most of his fright and allowed him to renew his concentration, to drill an opening big enough to squeeze through.

So intent was he on the final few centimeters, he ignored the light that snapped on in the observation cubicle, and the two faces peering down at him. By the time he did stop to take notice, he had finished drilling. Master Arnaud and Prentice Jady watched him. Jady scowled, her face contorted and even more unpleasant in that configuration.

But Master Arnaud's disapproving expression contained no surprise.

Eldon pushed and prodded the excised rectangle just enough so he could remove it, careful not to let it come in contact or damage the crystal flower.

Why hadn't they sounded the alarms? Eldon had no time to ponder that. Grabbing his pack from the floor, he stepped through the opening he'd made, looked once more at the observers, and reached out a hand to the arranged white flower. Here, close to the matrix, he detected a faint odor of salt and metal with an overlay of something more exotic, essential oil.

He grasped the nearest bloom.

A deep emptiness clawed at his stomach, then he couldn't feel his extremities, then any parts of his body, and then–

Eldon stumbled. Stretching out an arm to steady himself, he was surprised when his flailing hand hit something. A cold solid surface, a wall. Doubt and fear returned, dancing around in a fuddled brain that couldn't seem to orient itself. Was his body made of three or four or eleven dimensions? He wiggled his fingers and they seemed to be normal, but would his brain automatically adjust if they weren't?

In the quiet darkness, lit only by the faint glow from his goggles, something cracked, forcing Eldon's head up. Again a sharp crack, like breaking glass, but this time farther away, and followed by a faint echo. *Don't forget to breathe.*

He detected a lighter area straight ahead. Maybe traveling scrambled the senses and it took time to readjust. Or maybe the transition to an other-dimensional state was one his optical nerves were not equipped to deal with. But he didn't *feel* other-dimensional. His legs worked normally, and as panic receded, Eldon took a few steps forward until he reached the end of a short corridor.

A quick glance behind reassured him the crystal matrix from which he'd entered was still there. Had it traveled with him? Did it transcend some sort of boundary? The blossoms tempted him to touch them again, the essential oil smell stronger. But Arnaud's scowl and Jady's unfeminine grimace lay in that direction. The corridor glowed faintly, like the sun about to come up.

How much time did he have before they came after him?

The walls appeared to be made of plaster, damaged and peeling, the floor littered with fallen fragments.

The floor below him shifted and split as tendrils of brownish-black crystal as thick as his arm and covered in hair-like tendrils rose and fell in a not-so-gentle undulation. A shaggy crystal serpent snaking its way along the corridor. The jerky movements of the crystal were also the source of the cracking sounds as the tendril forced its way through the floor.

Could it be a crystal root? Was the cracking due to a change in temperature? Eldon didn't recall that their crystal matrix had been sensitive to the small range of temperatures that humans endured.

He didn't feel cold or warm, just alert; it was as if his body was just there, embedded in its environment. His lab coat was coated with a layer of plaster dust. He shed it and shrugged into the supple fleece anorak he drew out of his pack.

The 'root' followed a path to where it joined with the crystal flower matrix he'd just come through, adding weight to the idea the structure was growing. But was it alive? Normal crystals weren't alive. But these crystals, in many ways similar to those within the earth's interior that over geologic time resulted in rocks and minerals and precious gems, were very different. They grew and evolved, powered by a core of quantum foam. Eldon scoffed at the idea that anything so beautiful could be considered lifeless.

And how had this corridor formed if not through growth? All of us–them–the engineers, physicists, chemists, and bio geoscientists–had certainly not planned or simulated anything like this. The matrix grew. But what was it growing into? Was Eldon still within the matrix and imagining all this? He would know if he had transcended the three geometrical dimensions humanity called space–surely, it would be different than this–but what about time, the fourth dimension? Was that the factor that had altered?

Diffuse light also bled in from the ceiling, which appeared open but was too high to tell. But to what was it open? He removed his goggles and waited for his eyes to adjust to semi-darkness. Those goggles had felt uncomfortably tight, reminding him of confinement… best not to think about that now. He breathed out easier.

Shrugging on his pack and pulling it secure on his shoulders, Eldon took tentative steps toward the end of the corridor. Eldon stepped through into a large round enclosure.

Arranged around the perimeter were twelve recessed arches. All except one held crystal matrices just like the one grown at the project. Three additional–opposite and adjacent–corridors opened onto other spaces. Two lines connecting them would bisect the large hall into four neat triangles, pie pieces, each with three arches as toppings. He automatically numbered them clockwise as quadrants one, two, three and four.

The corridor in quadrant two resembled a small unkempt arboretum, as if abandoned to its own overgrowth, the ground ruptured between masses of root and, yes, they looked like weeds. Decidedly charming crystal weeds.

But here in the main hall, eleven crystal blossoms nestled in their separate arches bled out a creamy sorbet light, permeating the space with a subtle glow. The arch in quadrant four was dark and empty.

Eldon smiled and a giggle escaped. It was a goddamn crystal *glade*, with each matrix a doorway to… the only thing he could think of was even though he hadn't transcended known space, he was somewhere different to everywhere else, to all he had ever known.

He revised his earlier assessment.

This was the most captivating thing he was ever likely to see. Here in the midst of a crystal transit glade. Sorbet Junction, he christened it.

He barked a laugh that echoed, and then shook his head No passing marks from a psych test were needed to appreciate this. His night terrors caused by fading memories of a broken childhood as a captive of a fanatic religious cult caused him occasional problems; but here, now, he functioned as well as anyone. Perhaps, even better.

Eldon rarely ventured outside the walls of the institute. He had known happiness within its walls and never wanted that to change. Until it did. If they hadn't kicked him out of the project, he might never have had the courage to do this, to enter a foreign world, foreign in a way he could never have imagined. It was too soon for him to fret about his newfound status of being somewhere else.

Eldon had been one of the prime candidates for testing the matrix. He'd seen his name one day in Master Arnaud's notebook along with Jenkins and another man, one of the geologists. They'd both disappeared sometime afterwards and never been heard from again. Had those men also been mustered out as rudely as he had been? He remembered Jenkins as being nice. Dedicated and not haughty. Or mean.

Eldon quickly examined the corridor in quadrant two, the weedy one. Except for the explosive growth of the matrix here, it matched the one he'd entered from, the crystal flower a complete duplicate, although there were differences in the root- choked floor. The environment presented as chaotic compared to the corridor he'd come in on.

So, eleven crystal matrices–the missing one would have been number twelve–for the main hall. Plus four in the corridors. Sixteen doorways? But what did it signify? Parallel worlds? It didn't seem many for myriad universes, the fabled multiverse, spoken of in hushed whispers by the physicists afraid of being labeled as pseudoscientists. Perhaps the arches led to other transit glades, who knew, but given enough time and sufficient exploration, he could find out.

Time was a commodity he just didn't have. For the present, he'd have to settle for insufficient, ad hoc exploration. Settle? That was good. Soldier onward, grit his teeth and do it, those were the right emotions for what he was about to attempt.

Arnaud and Jady would come. They were probably readying a team right now while he dithered. He pictured them cursing his name, not so secretly envious of his historic first trip. They'd want to bring him to justice and then explore the transit glade for themselves.

Taking quick strides to the center of the main hall, Eldon examined each of the eleven arches and their crystal lattice trees. They looked the same. Exactly the same. He couldn't see any differences. Did it reflect an underlying law of physics; was this the only way they grew, so unlike real crystals whose growth had an intrinsic chaotic element? No two crystals on earth were alike, despite their fundamental crystal lattices, rhombic, square, hexagonal, etc.

The empty arch in quadrant four, the first arch next to his entry corridor, devoid of its sorbet crystal flower, represented the only flaw in the symmetry of this bewildering place. He forced himself to go for a closer look.

Picking his way over the intervening roots and rubble, he marveled again at the light source. The arboretum's wall reached at least five meters. The diffused light oozed down from above and made it hard to ascertain structure. Power flowed from somewhere despite an eerie but pervading sense of abandonment or decay. That gave him hope the crystal trees, he'd already begun thinking of them as transit trees, were active.

He stumbled, sprawling over the uneven floor, his cheek landing against broken tiles. Small shards of crystal cut his face. Blood trickled.

Pulling himself to sit, his knees raised in front of him, Eldon wiped away the blood and then probed the shallow cheek cuts and one on his toe. The trekking sandals had not been a good idea. His legs and arms felt whole. Bruised maybe, like his ego.

Sturdy hiking boots, that would have been the thing. He glanced to the side, taking deep breaths. Standing on shaky legs, Eldon saw something jutting up between two adjacent roots in front of him.

It appeared to be a rectangle of white fabric. He couldn't reach it from where he sat, so he took two steps. The fabric resisted, stuck between two crystal roots grown over it. The small square of linen mesh, just longer than both his hands and a little bit wider than one, was of a loose weave, soft but sturdy. It contained writing which bled into the warp and weave. A salty metallic odor, similar yet different to the scent of the crystal matrix assaulted his nostrils. A tangy smell, like the blood on his cheeks.

Eldon tugged harder. The fabric still didn't come loose. He pulled with both hands. It came away, sending him stumbling back. He waved his arms to gain his balance, a nerdy reaction; he was glad no one watched. He breathed hard and looked at his prize.

Whoever had left it here, had written this on purpose, had wanted to communicate something. At this rate, he'd solve the whole puzzle in about two lifetimes, three at the latest.

Who had torn a piece from a shirt or a cloak or… a lab coat… and written on it in a hasty script? He rotated it, seeking an orientation that made sense. It was a map of the circular hall and the corridors, each crystal flower marked with tiny flower heads. Several of the flowers had an 'x' through them.

There was no writing, just symbols, one for each of the crystal flowers and one symbol for each of the four corridors, and some of them looked immediately familiar. Others, he'd need to think about. Eldon had once made a study of symbols. It was when he had been imprisoned and punished by the cult for his rebellion of attempted escape Without any other outlet but to study the things he was allowed to have in his tiny cell… but he didn't want to think about those days right now.

Holding the cloth out further didn't help. Until Eldon remembered the tiny flashlight in his pack. He dug it out and shone it on the fabric. One symbol was used mainly but not exclusively by Celtic peoples. One flower was marked with a rune, possibly Germanic. He shook his head. The mark had the quality of a rune, long lines and angular shapes, but it wasn't Germanic or Nordic. He'd once practiced writing poetry with elder Futhark and knew its permutations well. A few of the others looked oriental – Chinese or Japanese – and he'd have to look at them closely to be able to differentiate. There were Greek, Mycenaean, and Hebrew letters. And a few he couldn't clearly identify but could have been symbols from other cultures.

Eldon folded the cloth carefully and stuck it into one of his many pockets. The 'x' on four of the crystal matrices had to have something to do with the workability of the crystal transit or–and this thought worried him the most–a warning to stay away.

He swiped his hands along his cargo pants, now dirty after his fall. Heavier pants would have suited better. He zipped up his fleece and kinked his neck. How much time did he have left? Eldon was honestly bewildered why the others hadn't already come through to try and stop him.

But at least he had a road map of sorts for Sorbet Junction. Which one of the transit trees to try? Interesting that the cloth had been left in front of the only obliterated crystal matrix. He shone his flashlight among the debris. Maybe there were more clues.

At the spot where he'd found the cloth, there was something. He had to kneel again to see it and then he wished he hadn't.

A forefinger, decidedly human, lay in the space under where the fabric map had been. Fighting back bile, he picked it up. It felt cold, the skin hardened by exposure, and an unpleasant shade of gray, the fingernail surprisingly clean. The skin did not look used to hard manual labor. Eldon had seen what skin looked like in that condition. Rough and worn and pale.

Unable to physically hold back the pain of those distant memories, he turned and retched bile. He felt a little better for it. Eldon wiped his mouth and thought about taking the finger with him, a mute companion on his further trials. His mind flitted over the possibilities and he came up with one unassailable in its logic.

Eldon was not the first explorer from the Institute of Applied Biomathematics to travel through the crystal matrix.

He let the finger lie where it was. A grave of sorts. The rest of the person must have perished in the explosion that destroyed the crystal bloom. Eldon looked around some more, shining his light about, nervous about finding additional remains. But there wasn't anything visible on the surface except the crystal shards he'd tripped over earlier.

It was time to move on.

Eldon took out the fabric map again, smoothing it with his fingers. He wished whoever had drawn it would have put an x over *the* crystal matrix. *The* One he should take. Stare as he might, he couldn't decide whether one was better than another. But going back now would not only be pointless, it would be madness.

He thought about Jenkins and the other man who'd gone missing. No one had seen or heard from them after their disappearance, and everyone, Eldon included, assumed they'd left the institute altogether, never to be heard from again. The I.A.B.M. was insular, incestuously so. Those who studied and worked there lived there, for the most part, and had few contacts outside of institute life. Eldon had none whatsoever. He'd never even regretted that, content as he was to be a part of it, to have been accepted into a family where he was happily anonymous yet part of a dynamic whole, working together on projects such as this one.

Time was not a commodity he possessed, he reminded himself, and swiped a finger over the fabric. If this was a message, a riddle, then he had to think clearly and quickly. The symbols he could identify he ruled out as possibilities. The ones that seemed familiar but that he couldn't readily identify he also ruled out. Instinct poking him again.

That left only one transit tree. The one with the altered, unfamiliar rune. He took the fabric square with him to the center of the main hall and after turning it in each of the four possible configurations, decided with a hefty portion of guessing and the location of the blown-to-bits transit tree, that the chaotically overgrown arboretum corridor and the one with the altered rune were one and the same.

But before committing to the next step, to the possibility of being blown to bits with only a partial finger as a testimony to his former existence, he marched back down the corridor in quadrant one, the corridor from which he'd come.

Before he got the end, he stopped, a scream escaping.

The bloom had exploded, crystal fragments littering the floor. The arch stood empty and dark. He thought of Jenkins again, now more than certain he needed to find out what had happened to the Map Man. Another part of him just wanted to curl up and pretend it all hadn't happened.

The way back home no longer existed. That also explained why he hadn't been followed. The transit was closed. The tree destroyed.

Eldon gurgled stupidly and sank to the floor. No Jady to chase him or Master Arnaud, but no one else either. No one he'd known or who knew him. He was alone. Forever alone.

But at least he was not confined to a tiny cell.

Eldon grasped the fabric in a closed fist and marched over to the weed-infested arboretum. He breathed heavily, railing against his fate. But then thought it was the best and only choice.

He reached up to cup one of the blooms in his hand and closed his eyes. An elongated cry sounded – as of someone shouting from a moving train – and cut off as he was swept away.

The crystal matrix embraced him.

Eldon fought panic as he came to. But he wasn't locked in a cell in the bowels of the cult headquarters. He wasn't being punished for trying to escape. The man and the woman who'd rescued him and set him free shone bright in his memory. They were the ones who'd secured him his place in the institute, and he would be forever grateful to them.

How long had he been asleep? Eldon felt for his blankets, then realized he wasn't in a bed. He laid in tall grass under a deep blue sky with a sun not very high in the sky with a promise of warmth. It was indeed morning.

His stomach gurgled. Eldon needed nourishment. Or a reasonable coffee substitute. The air smelled clean and fresh. The earth moist and rich. He clutched a strip of fabric in his hand and remembered. He'd gone through the crystal matrix, the blossom that looked like lemon sorbet and smelled of machine shop liberally dosed with incense or patchouli or lavender oil. Shivery cold crawled over his arms, but not unpleasantly so.

He sat and looked around. The crystal flower matrix appeared different here, nearly invisible if one didn't know what to look for. Just a couple of meters away from him, nestled within a field of similar creamy blooms – sunflowers – the crystal bloom was indeed hidden. Eldon had never seen creamy sunflowers before, those only in pictures, but he did recognize the essential oil fragrance that emanated from them as a part of the smell of the matrix itself. Had they been planted there on purpose?

A plume of smoke curled upward in the distance beyond the sunflower field. He stood and started walking that way, taking bold strides.

He was in a new world.

It did not transcend the familiar four dimensions. There was breadth, height and width. Time passed because the sun rose perceptibly higher and a few wispy clouds moved across the sky.

He reached the encampment after what felt like only a short time. This experience, of being outside, no buildings, no visible civilization, nothing to confine him, not yet anyway, made Eldon's chest expand rather than shrink. If he could find sustenance and something to slake his thirst, he would give in to growing optimism.

A single teepee of animal hides attached and held up by shaved sticks made him stop. The fire had burned down to smoky embers. But no one was here. Beyond the encampment was a grove of trees, not crystal, not of the transit variety at all. Just trees. Eldon didn't have names for them. They promised silence and concealment should he require it.

But before Eldon could hide himself within the safety of bark and leaves and a multitude of trunks, he heard a branch crack and whirled around.

A man dressed in animal skins similar to the ones the teepee was made out of stood there and aimed a crude bow and fletched arrow at him. One of his forefingers was missing. Eldon opened his mouth but no sound came out. He closed his eyes and hoped it would be quick. Better than most ways to end it, he thought. He'd come farther than he thought he would.

"Bakker?" the man asked. "Eldon, isn't it?"

Eldon opened his eyes, one at a time. Giddiness came over him. Jenkins stood before him. His dark skin gleamed in the sun. His once close-cropped hair now had a wild curly look to it.

"I found your map. And your finger... but... you're not blown up." His voice sounded rusty and cracked to his ears. Eldon took the map out of his pocket and showed it to Jenkins.

Jenkins lowered the bow and grinned. "I knew it. If anyone could have figured it out enough to follow me, then it would have been the right clue. Welcome to the New World. Are you hungry?"

Eldon told his story while wolfing down strips of deer jerky and drank cold tea from a cracked ceramic teacup he and Jenkins shared. Jenkins listened while sharpening arrowheads with a rough piece of slate, pausing to test each carefully.

They sat cross-legged in front of Jenkins' teepee. Jenkins used a crude bellows made also of hides and sticks to fan the fire back into life and then thrown a few sticks onto it. Eldon didn't feel he needed the warmth as much as when he woke, what seemed like an age ago but was probably only about an hour or two.

When Eldon finished the jerky and his tale, Jenkins sighed and sat back.

"Where are we, Jenkins?" Eldon asked.

Jenkins left the camp without giving an answer. When he returned a few moments later, he carried a dented metal pan. Stones pulled from the fire served as a base for the pan. Jenkin's missing right fore-finger had scarred over, but it still looked red and angry.

"I don't know," Jenkins said finally. "My name is Andrew. Call me Andy."

"What happened to you… Andrew… Andy?"

"Mine is a similar tale to yours. Except I wasn't duped into going into the crystal flower. Arnaud threatened me directly. They wanted me to look for Reneer. It seems he really did go on a walkabout without permission."

"Duped? You think–"

"Yes. You were set up. They wanted you to come and look for me."

"Jady. They used her."

Andy laughed. "Used Jady? She's Arnaud's daughter."

Eldon stretched his lips in a line. He didn't know whether he could trust Jenkins… Andy… but why would he lie to him? It just didn't make sense. But, it did make sense. In a weird way. Andy busied himself with the pot, stirring the bits and pieces of plants he'd thrown in.

"Reneer. Is that the other man who went missing? We all assumed you'd been kicked out of the institute. No one ever told us why or what happened."

"Did you ask?" Andy asked, his tone condescending.

Eldon shook his head. "No, of course not. None of us were that brave."

"Brave little braves," Andy said.

"I'm sorry. We were all such naïve bastards."

"They listed us as missing?" Andy shook the pan and then used a crude sieve to strain the liquid into their teacup.

At least Andy had thought to bring a few essentials with him. Eldon had only brought the tiny flashlight and a plastic thermos of water. Naïve bastard for sure. He'd just assumed that when he went through the crystal matrix, the universe would take care of him. Right. Just like it always had.

"That was the rumor that circulated. Probably was fed to us, like everything else." Eldon sat back after taking a sip of tea and passing the cup again. "But, I just don't understand."

Andy drank tea and sighed. "You need to drink a lot. It's more important than food. What don't you understand?"

"Any of it. If they knew about the transit glade... I named it Sorbet Junction... knew that it led to places like this." Eldon gestured around him. "Why didn't they just tell us?"

Andy laughed. "Glade, huh? Sorbet Junction. That's an excellent name. I just called it the hall of crystal flowers. Very imaginative of me."

"I had... still have no idea what all of this is. My hypothesis was the matrices all led to parallel universes."

"You're not far wrong there," Andy said.

"But... Arnaud sent you out? He must have trusted you."

"Reneer and I were his first and best pupils. We were the original coordinators of the so-called 'transdimensional' project. We knew it was anything but. But we were otherwise clueless as well. After everything was up and running, we went out first. And we came back to report about it. It was all very secret." Andy paused to sip tea.

"Arnaud may be a bastard but he's not stupid. And he didn't trust anyone. Except Jady. He thought we were all out to steal his great discovery, the crystal matrix. So he kept everything to himself. He trusted Reneer at first. But Arnaud figured out Reneer probably was out to steal his secrets. I never got a chance to talk to him to find out the truth. When I caught up to him, he was already dead. It took me a while to return." Andy grimaced and shook his head. "By then, Arnaud had adjusted his way of doing business with the rank and file Prentice. He learned from his mistake with us…"

"But I thought *you* were the one who was blown up," Eldon said.

"Nearly was. Lost my finger just after I found Reneer's body… when I escaped through the crystal back to the… glade but lost all my supplies in my flight. The darn thing exploded. They do that once you go back through. Inconvenient as all heck."

Eldon let out a sigh, already nostalgic for his former life, his soft bed and his blankets, a comfortable chair in the library with all the books a young man could want. He could learn everything he needed to know about life just from books.

"So you built the transit glade? With Reneer?"

Andy laughed again and it sounded only a bit hysterical. "Yeah. That's the cool part. We didn't. When we went through the crystal the first time…" Andy looked at him keenly.

Eldon swallowed. "What?"

"That construction – the corridors, the arches with the other flowers, all of it – *it was already there.*"

Eldon handed Andy the linen map he'd found and, Andy explained what he had figured out. "Each of the flowers leads to a different period in our – homo sapiens – past. Each period is one dominated by a different religion. We call them mythologies now. Most of them. But at one time they were what people believed in. Time machines to humanity's religions and superstitions. I don't know if they're true to history as we know it. My hypothesis is that they're alternate branches where each of those religions dominate. But who knows for sure? I'm just one man. And Reneer is dead."

Time machines! That was something Eldon hadn't considered. He felt a great sense of awe. And excitement. "You've been to all of them?"

"No, not all. Reneer probably explored as well. The flowers explode when you go back through. But after a time, they're there again. As if they regrow from the roots that snake all over the place."

"But I thought–"

"You thought the crystal flower you saw at the institute was the first one?" He guffawed. "Arnaud. What a magician. He kept pulling crystal flowers out of his hat instead of rabbits. And no one the wiser."

"After all the exploration, all you had was this?" Eldon gestured at the crude fabric with the smeared out symbols.

Andy shrugged and looked off to the right. "After losing my finger and with Reneer gone, I decided not to go back to tell Arnaud. This here, this was one of the places where I hadn't met any natives who either wanted to enslave or kill me. It seemed like a good place to end up. I just have to learn how to survive a little better."

"And why the map?"

He shrugged again. "I figured someone else would be along and find it. The chances they'd end up here were not too bad. Sixteen to one, to be more precise."

Something about Jenkins' story didn't add up. Something big he wasn't letting Eldon in on. And Eldon had enough of being duped.

"The crystal leading back to the institute exploded. I wouldn't have been able to go back through. But I'd only been through once."

Andy nodded. "Logic. Someone else came and went. And boom!" Andy clapped his hands.

Eldon didn't like what the conclusion portended. He'd been watched. "And so that's your plan? Survival?"

"For now. What's your plan, Eldon?"

Eldon stared at the crude map and wondered where Jenkins... Andy... kept the real one and what he planned on doing with it. He'd have to gain his trust before he asked again. Jenkins didn't plan on going back to the Institute for Applied Biomathematics. Or the world they'd both come from. He couldn't anyway since the crystal that led back to the institute had exploded. However long it took to regrow from this end... would it also have to be built again from the other end, by Master Arnaud and his clueless team of Prentices?

Well, they were less one Prentice now. Eldon didn't want to go back either. But he didn't know if he was ready to stay forever. Was this the best his imagination had to offer? It was. For now.

And Eldon did know one thing. He needed better equipment. And a look at that map. He'd spent most of his formative years captive to the group of religious fanatics that included his parents. After rebelling and and being punished over and over again, he had ultimately been rescued before being permanently damaged. The scars remained in the form of fear of certain things, like being confined. Eldon hated small spaces. And he hated being alone. He certainly didn't want to wander into anybody's past religion and have to go through something like that again. Or worse. There was always worse. Ask Reneer.

Whether Jenkins proved trustworthy, he would have to find out. At least he hadn't put an arrow through Eldon's head.

Nearly burned down, the fire crackled. Andy put his arrows into a cloth sack he slung on his back and shouldered his bow.

"What I don't understand is the symbol you drew for this place. It's not a real rune, is it? Nordic or Germanic. I know those runes. But it's similar."

Andy smiled. "You're smart. I just made up the symbol. The Germanic and the Nordic crystal matrices blew up a while back. They were down those other two corridors. Could have stayed in either of them, I guess. Except for my skin color." He looked away again.

Eldon sighed.

Andy nodded and stood. Eldon stood with him although he didn't know what they were going to do now or where they were going. "And what does that mean... you made it up?"

Andy pointed to the grassy plains, to the sky, to the horizon that stretched out before them. "No religion. It's just here and now and wide open spaces."

"The transit to atheism then?"

"Could be. Maybe that's why there's no natives here. No people, no beliefs. Except us now. We can believe anything we want to."

"Is that why the weeds grew? The garden run wild." Eldon's thought came out loud.

Jenkins crossed his arms and waited.

Eldon asked, "Us? As in you and me?"

"I'll tell you a secret."

Eldon nodded. "Go on."

"You want to go back?"

Eldon nodded. "To get things."

"Not a bad idea." Jenkin's smile was rueful. "If you try to go back, even if it's just to bring things, well, it doesn't work that way."

"Why not?" Eldon looked down at his trekking sandals. They'd be pretty good here, but he wanted socks too. And books. And maybe some other stuff. A pillow would be nice. And someone like Jady, of the female variety. He hated to admit it, but it was true.

"The flowers go to a different place when they regrow. Maybe the same mythology, I'm pretty sure about that, but a different branch. You can't go back to the same place twice."

"Not even the institute?"

"It's there all right. And Arnaud is there, and it might look like the same place. But it's not. You don't exist there, at least not the same you, although there's certainly someone like you or there was."

"And that means I have to either stay here and be alone with you or chance being completely alone somewhen else or go back to an institute where I no longer exist except as a stranger-me. That's creepy. And it's a pretty good secret."

"Here's the secret. *I'm not alone.*"

"What?"

"I enticed a few others here. Like you. We're starting over."

Eldon wondered how much Andy Jenkins wasn't really telling him. How much Jenkins had to do with his being here, rather than it being any master plan of Master Arnaud's.

But then he decided it didn't matter. Not now. Maybe later.

He told Jenkins he thought it would be much safer if they could blow up the flower so no one else could get in. Jenkins looked him over carefully and then kicked sand into the fire.

"It's okay if others come. Really," Andy said. "You came. And that's okay, too."

Eldon wondered what winters were like here. Whether there was snow. Where the others lived. Had anyone thought to bring books? They'd need to write new ones. Learn everything all over again. But one thing was missing. For sure.

"There's something I want to figure out how to make," Eldon said.

"What's that?" Andy asked.

"Lemon sorbet," Eldon said. "I seem to have acquired a craving for it."

Jenkins' puzzlement was followed by an enthused grin. A good symbol of things to come. It was a wide world, Andy had said.

And Eldon really wanted to get a look at that map. With it, he never needed to be confined to a single world.

AA JANKIEWICZ

 A.A. Jankiewicz (known to most as Agnes) hails from the city of Pickering, Ontario. Her debut novel Q-16 and the Eye to All Worlds was published as part of her thesis project at Durham College for the Contemporary Media Production Program. Prior to that, she graduated from York University with a BFA in Film Theory, Historiography and Criticism. When she's not busy plotting the next great adventure, writing, doodling, tinkering in the Adobe suite of programs, or mellowing out with her friends, she enjoys walks with her four-legged companion Meesha. She is currently working on the next installment in the Q-16 series.

THE SPACE DRIVER

By AA JANKIEWICZ

Subtly it floated. Suspended in a ghost-like drift through the air, the once well-loved stuffed brown bear moved past the window of the cargo ship. The vessel, a hulking leviathan of silver metal capable of moving three hundred thousand pounds, belonged to a fruit harvesting company on Earth known as C-tron. While the spacecraft could usually be seen going over eighty-seven thousand kilometres an hour, a blur to the human eye, it now rested at a standstill. In one of the windows, a pale light shone dimly.

Inside, a three-dimensional projection of a woman played out. She appeared to be in her mid-thirties, with light auburn hair and forget-me-not blue eyes which were alive with the smile spread across her diamond-shaped face. A black and white summer dress adorned her rippling from the ocean breeze around a pair of slender legs that chased a toddler, a boy in a pair of swim shorts with hair colour the same as her own, down a strip of white sandy beach. Catching up to him, she scooped the boy into her arms, blowing a raspberry into his tummy.

"You see daddy there, Owen?" the woman asked the boy and pointed ahead of herself, to which the boy seemed to freeze and then get excited at the prospect of seeing his other parent.

"Hey, squirt!" a male voice came out of nowhere, causing the boy to laugh, bringing his hands up to his face to hide his redness. "You having a good time?"

Owen, looking at his father, took a moment before he answered with a very cheerful nod, causing the voice of the man to laugh.

"See, I told you," he chuckled. "And you were so scared of the jellyfish. Didn't I tell you there weren't any in the water?"

The boy grimaced, causing both the man and woman to giggle some more.

Sighing, the man continued. "Oh, isn't this great Shannon? Tell me this isn't great?"

"It's great, hun, and you were absolutely right for taking us here," she replied as she moved closer to the camera.

She stayed that way for a few seconds, the water which surrounded them nothing more than a glimmering reflection in her eyes.

"I love you, Rob," she smiled.

"I love you too, Shan."

The projection froze and ended there, leaving Robert Addison the only living soul in the room. The lights came up, bringing him back to the reality of the white-walled and sterile environment of the ship. It was a setting he knew well from his many years of space driving, a term coined due to cargo ships transporting items much like trucks once did before the age of the colonies.

Knowing nothing else would come on, Robert sighed, turned around, and headed back for the cockpit. On his way out, he glanced at the communication device on the wall opposite of the door and, seeing no flickering light, he left. Winding down the narrow corridor and down a ladder from the upper levels, he slid back down into the black synthetic leather seat. Checking all the vitals of the ship, he paused to catch a reflection of himself on one of the touch screen surfaces. From beneath his bushy ape-like brows he could make out the faint tint of his hazel eyes. His triangular jaw now held a fortnight of facial hair on it and his russet-coloured wavy hair was disheveled, not having been combed. He felt there was no need for it, being the only one on board. Who would actually care?

It had been a mentality he'd been in for a long while now, and staring out into the depths of space, he was reminded why. He was reminded of the life that had been out there, before him. All that remained now was rock, static and memories. It all seemed another lifetime ago.

"Nothing to see I haven't seen," he muttered to himself in a gruff voice, the sounds of the words making no sense to him in the aftermath of speaking them.

He frowned and noting how cool the ship was, he pulled on his black polyester/cotton mix work jacket with the yellow C-tron logo sewn over the left side of his chest with his surname printed neatly below it in a smaller font.

Seeing everything was in order, he got up to resume his other duties. Climbing back up the ladder of the ship and moving down another set of corridors, accompanied only by the metallic sound of his gravity boots and breathing, he paused before an air tight sealed door. Looking to his right where a black glass panel could be seen, he pressed his hand against it. Red and blue LEP lights danced to life, scanned the hand, and displayed the name of the owner.

Sliding aside, the door revealed a white room the length of a football field filled with lemon trees. While many companies simply froze their off-world cargo, C-tron prided itself in delivering fresh products of the highest quality. What better way than to have it picked right off the tree when it arrived before being shipped off to homes? That was their way. The fruit to be used in juices, on the other hand, still came frozen to allow for bigger shipments.

Robert walked past the rows of lush green-leaved trees which were loaded with yellow fruit. Running a hand down one of the coarse skins of the fruit, he felt the heat of the artificial sunlight on them. Taking a deep breath, he smelled both the lemons and the earthy tones of the soil which lay spread all over the floor. After completing his walk around, he left.

The descent into the cockpit the second time around seemed longer. His boots appeared to weigh more than they should have. His whole frame, in fact, standing at a hundred and seventy-eight centimetres, felt more burdened than ever as it sank one last time into the chair. Laying his arms out over the worn faux leather armrests and taking a deep breath, he looked out into the depths of space before him. Opening the camera app on his screen, he pressed record, a little red dot appearing in the corner as his image became present on it.

"This is cargo space driver Robert Addison signing on," he began. "Though I don't know who is listening at this point. The time... well... it doesn't matter either, I suppose. What I am here to say is this will be my final recording, and it has been an honour to work for C-tron all of these years. To my family – wherever you may be – Owen and Shannon – I love and miss you both."

He searched inside himself for anything else he wanted to add. It seemed each time he had thought of this recording, he had monologues upon monologues stored away in his head. Now, when the time came, there was nothing. Nothing but static and the numbness that accompanied it.

Furrowing his brows, he tried to focus, but it was in vain. Giving up, he finally glanced back at the screen. "Goodbye."

Shutting off the camera, Robert looked into the corner of the cabin and reaching over, found a small, black briefcase. Opening it, he produced a pistol. It was a crude weapon, but one passed down to him from his great grandfather, who had served as an officer. He marvelled at the workmanship. It was a strange thing to know so small of a device could prove to be one's end. Perhaps that was the irony in it.

Loading the handgun and making sure the safety was off, he noted something in the corner of his eye. Glancing over at the many displays which showed video footage from the various rooms, he saw something moving in one of them. Letting out a growl of frustration, his sense of duty overriding all other emotions in him, he got up, putting the safety on the weapon once again as he climbed the ladder.

Trudging down the corridors again, he moved past the room where he inspected the trees and made his way further back. Coming to a rest at another door, he scanned his hand, then kept both hands on the weapon as he entered to find the entire room stacked with crates. The lighting was low to prevent any more heat than necessary from entering the facility, ensuring a constant temperature for the frozen fruit. The scent of lemons filled Robert's nostrils as he slowly paced through the room, his eyes focused as he scanned it for anything out of place. Nothing.

Lowering the weapon and allowing for the muscles in his shoulders to relax, he frowned. Perhaps his mind was starting to play tricks on him. Isolation tended to do that to one.

Content with the knowledge there was nothing amiss, he began to turn and make his way back. Hearing the sound of a crate crashing to the floor set off his inner alarm. Robert raised the weapon to eye level and pointed in the direction of the noise.

"Freeze!" he roared.

At first glance, Robert could see nothing amiss. He then looked down at the metal floor where a shadow at the far end of the room changed shape, elongating itself. Then the sound of shuffling feet. Followed by a teenage girl, no older than sixteen. She was unlike any Earth child Robert had ever seen. Small of stature with a thin frame made all the more prominent in the oversized grey worker jacket she wore, the girl had a round face, complete with a set of sapphire-coloured eyes. A piercing hung from the left side of her lower lip and her flaxen hair arranged into thick dreads cascaded well past her shoulders. What struck Robert most was the orange tint of her skin. The coloration did not occur where he came from, Earth. Farmers on Colony-537 who were exposed to excessive amounts of carotenoids in their food due the colony primarily harvesting fruits with a high concentration in them were prone to this trait. Sensing the girl meant no harm with her arms raised in the air, he lowered his guard a little.

"Who are you?" he demanded of her.

"My name's Talitha," the girl spoke timidly. "But everyone calls me Tali."

Internally upset at having his plans put on hold, Robert put the safety on the gun and stashed it in his coat pocket. He then turned his attention back to the girl. He motioned for her to come forward.

"You know, stowing away on an inter-colonial cargo ship is punishable by death right?" he asked, void of any emotion in his voice.

The girl looked down at her oversized boots, which were covered in dirt, while wrapping the jacket firmly around her. She looked back up at Robert, and he could see an unyielding resolve in her eyes.

"There was a war going on…" she began, trailing off mid-sentence.

Robert ran his hand through his beard as he analyzed the child. Colony-537 was perpetually in a state of war, mostly due to farmers being in constant conflict with the ruling classes there. The demand for fruit was constantly going up with ever-growing populations and with it, a demand for production farmers could not meet.

"There's always a war going on somewhere," he said with a frown.

"I need to get to Earth," she replied without any hesitation. "I can't go back there."

"Listen kid, you can't just go hopping on board cargo ships to do so," Robert retorted. "You need a passport, ticket, a full medical examination, and if you plan on staying anywhere for an extended period of time, a visa as well as a background check. You don't just up and go. There are regulations on that sort of thing."

"Please? I'll do whatever you ask," she begged. "I won't cause any trouble, just please don't send me back there."

Anger began to grow inside Robert. Who was this girl to think she could just barge in on him? He'd had it all planned out, how the entire day would go, and then she showed up.

"You can't go to Earth," he retorted once more. "Look, kid, it's not happening. I'm dropping you off at the nearest station and that's that."

"What difference would it make if you dropped me off on Earth?" she inquired. "I mean, really?"

"I'd be breaking protocol, would lose my license and my job as well," he stated, turning on his heel. "With me, to the cockpit where I can keep an eye on you."

"Who would find out, though? Just drop me off anywhere, I'll disappear and no one will find me," she continued.

Robert waited for her to leave the room and followed, locking the door as they left. He said nothing back, not feeling the need to reply to the last set of comments. In fact, all of the talking just seemed like more of the static he'd heard before, what did it all matter?

Coming down the corridor, Talitha stopped short of the final door separating them from the cockpit.

"You send me back there, I will have nothing," she spoke in a tone that was barely audible. "My whole family is dead."

The last part of the sentence seemed to pierce at the very core of Robert Addison. Like a piece of ice laid against fever-stricken skin. Scanning his hand on the wall, he opened the last set of doors to the cockpit, and going down the ladder, he revealed the field of debris before them.

"So is mine." The words seemed to tumble out of him.

Talitha cocked her head sideways, raised an eyebrow, and looked out through the windows, trying to make sense of what she saw.

Her thoughts were confirmed moments later. "The Earth was destroyed by an asteroid known as five thousand and seventy, or more commonly as Arai," Robert said. "What you see in front of you is what remains."

Talitha's orange face paled upon seeing the floating rocks outside. She walked up to the window, placing a hand on the surface.

"So, as I said before," Robert spoke again. "You can't go to Earth and neither can I."

The words trickled out of his mouth for the first time since he had realized the fate of the Earth. Till that point, it all seemed to be a bad dream, a figment of a nightmare he had yet to awaken from. Having to confront the girl with the news, however, brought the facts to life. The Earth was gone, and there was no coming back to it.

"I don't believe it. How did no one detect it? How did the colonies not hear anything about it?" She shook her head. "They have evacuation carriers for this reason, communication networks set up to contact people. I know there's one on this ship, people would have been patching through to say something."

"Too busy blowing each other up, I suppose." Robert crossed his arms as he looked out. "Too busy with their guns and their politics."

Talitha tightened the jacket around her. She looked over at Robert, who seemed to be staring out into space with glassy eyes, completely gone.

"They were there, weren't they?" she blurted out. "The woman and boy from the recording?"

Robert did not answer and proceeded to move forward, lowering himself into his seat. He flicked on all the needed switches and prepared for flight. A realization had dawned on him. He had no right to turn her in. He was, after all, a space driver.

Talitha sat down beside him in the passenger seat and fastened her harness.

"What's all of this going to mean for the colonies?" she asked.

Robert looked over at his companion. He was having a hard time processing the news as an adult, he could barely fathom what it was like to hear it as a child. Earth had always seemed indestructible. Part of him could not help but laugh at the irony of it all, even if the rest was mourning.

"I don't know," he answered. "I guess one of the larger colonies will assume control over the others. Or maybe they will all just drift apart now. I don't know, and I'm not deciding it. I'm just a driver."

Reversing out of where he had been stationed, Robert turned the ship around carefully, and proceeded forward. "How does Colony 542 sound?"

Talitha's eyes lit up, "You mean? I mean… yeah… sounds great."

The girl sank back into the chair and exhaled deeply. She stared into the blur of dark and stars as they passed before them, their velocity increasing with each second.

For the first time in a while, seeing the girl relax from the corner of his eye, Robert smiled a bit. He had been in that same spot for close to three weeks, never having moved and never having heard a single message. Despite this, he still went up each day to watch the recording he had. It had become part of his routine, the thing when kept him sane.

"Where will you go after?" Talitha continued the conversation, picking at a loose piece of pleather from the harness she wore.

"I don't know," he said to her. "I hadn't thought about it that far ahead."

The girl nodded and continued to watch the streaks of light pass all around them, like a psychedelic light show before speaking again. "When I was getting on the ship in the loading dock, I noticed there was some writing on the side of the ship. I couldn't make it out, the paint was very faded. What does it say?"

"It's the name of my ship. My wife's idea, she thought every ship needs to have a name, even a cargo ship," Robert answered her, keeping his eyes on the space before them.

"What did she call it?"

"Hope."

While the two conversed down below, attempting to soothe each other's wounds, somewhere up above, the light on the communication panel flickered.

DOUGLAS OWEN

An accomplished writer and content editor, Doug writes from the fantastical realms of Science Fiction and Fantasy to technical manuals and ISO instructions. He authors a column for IndyFest Magazine and is published through Ceder Cave Books, Mash Stories, and our own Science Fiction and Fantasy Publications imprint.

Doug holds certificates in creative and business writing and runs seminars where he teaches novel creation to people of all ages. He is also a NoNoWriMo winner for the last 5 years in a row. His latest accomplishment is completing the first draft of *Broken World: The Family* within seven days for the November 2017 NaNoWriMo with 64,000 words.

THE END OF THE WORLD

BY DOUGLAS OWEN

Time of Death

I lie on the bed with my eyes wide open, watching the time on my phone move towards 04:00 hours. For some reason it's hard to sleep. It has been that way for months. Nothing has changed in life, besides the ever present possibility of being called in for work early. That call has never been received, but for some reason, my thoughts keep telling me it will come.

04:00 hours arrives. No call. Nothing. I sigh with the relief that all will be well. My eyes can close once more. It's a chore to roll over and spoon without disturbing her. She has been patient with the wakeful nights. At least she doesn't mention it.

My phone rings.

I roll over and see the time, 04:02 hours. The office is calling. My perfect day is disrupted as the number flashes on the cell phone where it sits in the cradle. Why today?

The phone quiets as I grab it from the cradle. My feet find slippers, and without hesitation, out to the bedroom they lead me. The cat thinks I'm up to feed her and she rumbles down the stairs towards the kitchen. The bathroom is where I'm heading though.

"Hello?"

"Hello, Doctor Fergus?"

It really is a strange question when you come to think about it. This person has called my cell phone. Only two people live in this house and everyone knows it. So why do they believe someone else other than me would answer?

"Yes. The question, though, is who are you?" My voice is hushed, trying not to wake my wife.

"We have a 42."

You won't get the reference. Most people don't. It means someone found a planet killer.

"Are you sure?" Yes, I actually ask the question. Stupid, absolutely stupid. Of course he's sure. Why would he call if he wasn't sure?

"Yes, doc, we're sure. They verified it using Hubble."

"I'll be right in." Off goes the cell phone. There is scratching at the door and howling.

The howl turns to shock and is abruptly cut off.

"I got her."

I swear under my breath. The damn cat woke up the wife, and now she's going to want to know what's happened.

"I'm going to take a shower." My hand turns on the water. It thunders into the tub. "Go back to bed, I'll be home early."

"Let's get you some food." Her voice trails off.

I can hear her go downstairs over the sound of the water.

Get Going

The smell of coffee floats up from downstairs. God bless her, she turned on the pot. Every once in a while I'm surprised.

Clothes first. My hand hits the lights and there is my suit laid out for me with a bundle of fur on top of it. Reminds me of why I married her.

"Okay, Mitus. Off."

The cat just licks her leg. My head shakes. I reach out and move the queen out of the way in order to get dressed. It is 04:15 and time is running out. There is still another twenty minutes of driving ahead of me.

Mitus watches as I dress. She's my cat, and always wants to be near me. The stairs are close and once down them, I'm greeted with my wife's smile and a cup of coffee.

"I want you home early," she says, one hand holding her house coat closed and the other one smoothing my hair. She tugs at my beard. "You're getting a little salt in your pepper there."

"I love you too." I pull her close and kiss. She play-struggles and kisses me back. Arms hug me hard. "Hey, don't worry. Nothing's going to happen. Probably some big brass coming to see where the seven billion went this year."

"Yeah, right."

She can always tell when I'm lying, but what else is there to say? Honey, there's a huge asteroid, or even a rogue planet coming at us. Sure, that would go over really well.

She pushes away and gives me a stern look.

"Okay. I'll be back early."

She nods and gives me a peck on the cheek, then heads upstairs. The cat follows her.

"Love you."

"Love you too," she says.

I head out the door.

Just a Little One

It is still raining when I get out of the car. Not heavy, just enough to make you want to pull your clothes in around you. A rain that makes you shiver even though it's a mid-summer morning.

"Hi, doc." The guard recognizes me, but as usual I can't remember his name.

"Hi." My voice comes out like a squeak. The badge I carry slides over the reader and my smiling face is projected in front of the guard.

The holographic image is just one of those things I'm still not used to. And the capture they did is terrible.

"You're here early."

It's like he wants to know something but is afraid to ask. He knows our facility scans space for threats but what kind, he's not sure.

He opens his mouth and speaks again. "There's a whole lot'ta guys upstairs."

"Yeah, early. Just a routine inspection of the facility by some brass."

He smiles at that. Guess I'm not as good a liar as I thought. The guard nods me through.

"Mr. Brodden is near the lift. Could you remind him not to smoke in the building?" He pressed a button and magnetic locks disengage allowing me to enter the facility.

Sam is in the lobby, pacing. He looks tired. Circles paint a bluish brown under his eyes. He sees me, stops, and comes forward.

"You took your time."

I don't let him draw me into the argument. "What is it we have, Sam."

"A problem. Let's get up to Big Ben." He fishes in his pocket and comes up with a pack of cigarettes. A shaking hand fumbles one out and puts the cancer stick in his mouth. "Want one?"

"Thought you quit?"

His head shakes. "Who the fuck cares."

Sam lights up, blowing smoke out and coughing.

"Those things will kill you."

"Not fast enough." He hits the call button and we wait for the elevator. I hope that it takes a while. Sam in the elevator is bad enough. He has a restless leg. The cigarette is the other. It's been fifteen years since my last puff, and the smell usually makes me sick.

He sees me holding back and butts the thing out.

"Sorry, forgot."

The doors open and we enter. He hits seven and the doors close. I'm happy they killed the elevator music last month. It took a year, but all the emails finally sank in.

"Tell me a little about what was found." The silence is something I hate.

"I was told not to say anything."

"If this is a surprise party..." The last one they pulled was over a year ago.

"No." His answer is too short to be a lie.

"Then what?"

The elevator slows and stops. Doors open to the main room. At this time of the day it should be empty, but right now it's full. Twelve people are packed into it. My thoughts about this being a drill left me right then and there. Even the director is there talking with a man wearing enough medals on his uniform to build a small car. The scent of sweat fills the air along with a stale cigar.

"He's here," Sam calls out. The room quiets, and Carl, the director, looks over and motions for me to join him.

"About time you showed up," Carl says. "Looking for the dramatic entrance?"

The conference room doors open up. Julie stands there and looks over the group. Once her eyes land on me she comes forward. She looks worried.

"Hi, doc, everything's ready," she says, not a hint of the usual smile.

"What's going on, Julie?"

She hands over a binder. On the front are the words "Little One". My eyebrow rises. The code name is something I thought up.

Julie is standing there, nodding. I purse my lips and she turns, leading me into the conference room. Everyone follows.

Heat hits me as I enter the room. Big Ben must be working over-time. Air conditioners are throwing cold out, but processing power generates heat, and Big Ben has processing power to spare, or that's what we were told two years ago when we started this project. Now, I look at the readouts and see he's running at high capacity. It's the upper limit, allowing for basic commands to be run when needed.

"Ben," I call out. "What's your status?"

"Hello, doctor." They programed a baritone voice into Ben, but his inflections are always off just a bit. "I'm operating at 87.23% capacity.

CPUs 1-98 are calculating at 7.3 terahertz and the first seven banks of ram are dumping to disc. I'm 92% completed with the current calculations. Estimated time to completion is twelve minutes and thirty seven seconds."

Julie guides me towards a seat near the head of the conference table and makes me sit down. There's another binder on the table labeled "Out There". My mind reels. The title sparks something in the back of my skull, and it is itching there.

I go to open the binder and spy Carl shaking his head; he points to the binder Julie had given me. Thumbing through the binder makes my head pound.

There is a plotted course. A projected path through the solar system is laid out. Size is estimated with a surface area of 17 million square kilometers. Mass at over 1.67×10^{22} kg. Basically, it's the size of Eris. How did we miss it?

"Gentlemen," Carl says. "As you know we have a 42 alert. A planet killer."

Everyone starts talking at once. I scan through the binder for anything important. The heat is getting to me.

"Doc, you okay?" Carl asks.

I look up and see him staring at me. Concern is in his eyes.

"Yes, sorry. Just getting up to speed." My feet are under me quickly. "We have a planet killer coming at us. Preliminary information tells us it has the mass and size of Eris, our tenth planet, if you include dwarf planets. I always have. A planet is a planet. The trajectory shows we have three months at the object's current speed." I stop, and pinch the bridge of my nose.

"Ben, how far are you on those calculations?"

"Calculations are now finished, doctor."

Something tells me not to call them up. If it's not confirmed there is a chance it will not happen. There could be an error in the initial course projection, or maybe it's just a blob on the telescope.

No, I need to know for sure, and so does everyone else.

"Ben, display the data through the holographic unit in conference room one."

The table top glows briefly. Images in the form of the sun and planets are displayed. Each planet has its orbit shown. The main asteroid belt between Mars and Jupiter is also displayed along with the Trojan Asteroids, from the smallest rock to the largest boulder, tumbling in virtual space. Even the Kuiper belt encircles our solar system.

Just outside the Kuiper is a flashing dot. The date displayed is today's.

"I will move the time index forward." The days tick forward and the planets move about the sun. Little One moves forward through the Kuiper belt, striking several of the asteroids, spewing them into space. Thirty days and the rogue planet passes the orbit of Uranus, but the gas giant is on the other side of the sun. Thirty more days and the planet enters the asteroid belt, pushing its way from one side to the other, and making a tunnel through the orbiting debris field.

The asteroids from the Kuiper belt are striking planets and moons, throwing the small objects out of their own orbits. The planet wreaks havoc through the system. I shudder.

Three months, four days, nine hours and twenty-seven minutes later the rogue hits our moon. The display has increased in size to show the effects of the collision.

The moon pushes forward, the Little One having struck our only satellite square on. The collision slows the Little One slightly, delaying the strike, but the moon glances off Earth, taking a chunk out of the North Pole.

When the planet finally strikes Earth twelve minutes later, there is a cracking of the surface. Ben's voice interjects, "I have extrapolated the course of every object. The strike will happen within the shown time-line. Each spatial object is tracked from the start to finish. The destruction of Earth is predicted based on current knowledge of the planet's structure. I'm sorry, doctor." The planets dissolve and the calculations display before us. Reams of information flows as the computer dumps memory to make room for the next function we will ask it to perform.

Out There

Seven people sit with their mouths open. One runs to the door, probably trying to get to the bathroom, but fails. He vomits just as he exits the room. I watch a tear drop from Julie's eye.

"Doc," Carl said. "How accurate is this model?"

I know what he's doing. He wants a way out. Some type of possibility that the world will survive this disaster. It's unfortunate something like this could not be disregarded.

"Sorry, Carl, there's no mistake. Ben's got the biggest processing power available." I see my fingers playing with the binder labeled "Out There", and wonder what it is all about. "Remember Halley's comet? Ben's the one that predicted its destruction while everyone else predicted its return."

"I remember that, a few years before I came on board."

My eyes won't leave the binder now.

"Go ahead."

I look up and Carl's smiling. He's inclining his head towards the binder. I pull it towards me and start skimming it. My eyes widen in disbelief.

"When did this—" I start.

"It was my last directorship." Carl is grinning now.

"But when? How? Why haven't I heard of anything like this before?" My head is reeling now.

"I started project 'Out There' ten years ago," he says. "Each member of the United Nations has been syphoning money towards the project. Took us three years to get the plans drawn. Another four to build the facility. It surprised me how fast the parts came in. Some ordered through NASA, others from different country's space exploration arms. It was quite easy, really." His smile cuts through the cloud of people talking.

"Look," I say, standing. My body is craving fresh air. "I have no idea what this project's about. Really, the scale of this is phenomenal!" I'm waving the binder in front of me subconsciously. "How all of this was built without anyone knowing is just..."

"You skimmed it," he says to me. "There's no worry about it. Use the information and just follow the timeline on the last page."

The chime rings and Big Ben calls everyone back to the conference room. My hand turns the chair towards me, the tall, black back invites me to sit and be comfortable, but the feeling running up and down my spine is nothing like that.

"The floor is yours, Doctor." Ben turns off his speaker and I stand once again.

"It seems we have a way to survive, but not much time to do it in." I then start to lay out the plan in the binder.

Getting Ready

I can't believe how easily Julie transitioned from our small office to the big one in this new facility. The lack of windows unnerves me, personally. How people could work with the walls looming over them baffles my understanding.

Several other astrophysicists help me deal with all the details concerning the plan. This is beyond me. How did they think I could handle all the details involved? So much to do and so little time to do it in. Why couldn't we have found the 42 sooner? It really wouldn't have made any difference. We would have just pushed with less ferocity than we are now.

The piles of requisitions scream at me for attention. One finds its way in to my hands, and I read it with disinterest. Toilet paper, really? There has to be something else to ask for. Three tons, that's how much they're asking for. They must be elephants or something. What the hell would they be using that much for?

"Julie," I call out, hoping to pass on the need to investigate.

"Yes, doc?" she says when her face pokes into the room.

"Here." I hold out the requisition form to her. "Find out how many times section seven flushes the toilet and see if they really need so much ass-wipe."

She grabs the paper from me and chuckles. "I'll look in on it." I can see the question in her eyes.

"What?"

"Are you okay?"

"We've worked together for about twelve years now, right?" My fingers run thought my hair, scratching at an imaginary itch at the back of my skull.

"A little over, I'd say." Her eyes are full of concern.

"Have you even known me to be an administrator?"

She starts to giggle.

"Sorry, doc. It's just that for the last few days you've shuffled more paper and administrated this facility better than anyone. There's no one I could point to who would have done a better job." She flourishes the requisition form in front of her. "Most would have just signed off on this without even thinking."

My mind pictures Carl behind the desk with crates of toilet paper stacked behind him and I start to laugh.

"Carl, right?" Julie says.

"Yes. It's stacked—"

"—Behind him."

The headache starts to disappear. The levity is enough to break the ice. Standing, I make my way around the desk and take the requisition from her. "I'll take care of this."

She giggles her way back to her desk.

The hallway is inviting as a cave is to someone who's claustrophobic. I keep getting the sense that the world is about to collapse, and it's not that far off. We're all surprised that no one has found out our little secrete, that of the 42. Maybe that's what they needed the toilet paper for. Build a little bouncing point for the impact zone.

One door keeps me away from the head of software development. Someone had a sense of humour, taping 'Super Geeks' over the actual department name with a drawing of a classic geek with a cap blowing in the wind. The pocket protector is a cute touch.

I reach out and open the door. Seven people are grouped around the large window decorating the wall. It's unbelievable that they have windows in their area and there's none in my office. Things will have to change.

There's a name on the requisition form. A Marcus Kollof.

"Who's Marcus Kollof, and why does he need so much toilet paper?" My voice has the desired effect.

The group breaks up and each head for their chairs, all except one. The red haired gorilla just turns and scowls at me. A thick Russian accent breaks through his lips. "Who says I'm full of der'mo?"

I step into the room and walk towards the window. "The one who approves your seat on her." One finger of my left hand points to The Hope down below.

Very few people have ever seen The Hope. The ship is huge. Enough to hold five hundred people and all the supplies needed to make their trip to Gliese.

We have five such ships ready to reach out to the stars. Each with the same experimental drive system they claim will allow us to surpass the speed of light. The bulk of each ship's drive system is already in space, hidden in a polar orbit behind large shields. If people look for them they will just see a black field.

The blunt nose of each ship arches back to the sleek body, and two large pods reach out from both sides. They collect hydrogen and transfer it to the engine for burning. The lines are bold enough to get lost in, but each ship has a Big Ben installed in its head. Nothing will stop us from surviving. Nothing, that is, except sloppy programming.

"Or better yet," I say. "The paper here says you are."

Marcus steps forward and snatches the requisition form from my hand. "Explain."

"You've requested 3 tons of toilet paper—"

"No, delo." His finger jabs the paper, almost puncturing it.

"Tons. That's what is says here."

"Delo. See, you have to see the py."

"Look, you've spelled it ton, and I can't approve that much. Redo it and put it in English. See the top here? All requisitions must be in English." I reach over and point out the instructions to him.

"Der'mo meshok!"

"What?" I say.

"Shit bag. Computer translates poorly." He smiles now, the gap between his front teeth showing. "Me full of shit."

"Just correct it." I start to leave but his meat hook of a hand lands on my shoulder.

"You need to see." He guides me to the terminal at his desk. "You Big Ben work good, but issues with calculation."

"What do you mean?" Something is telling me this is important, but there is only so much one can do.

"I link all Big Ben together. Good spectrum here not used. New information shows planet speeding up. Time not much." His smile is gone now, and the readout on the terminal is spewing out numbers.

"When one Big Ben made for American calculate, it make pretty picture for all to see. Not much time on real numbers, just lines in air to make happy." I'm leaning in now, seeing the figures come to the correct assumption. We have less time than we predicted.

We Meet Again

I'm tired.

After a long four hours of analyzing the data Marcus showed there was no dismissing the information. The planet was speeding up. It's our sun, and it took the combined processing power of the Big Bens to figure it out. No fancy graphics, just numbers. Numbers and the gravity well of our star.

Once everything was collated, a fast jet was prepared and my bags magically appeared in the passenger compartment along with a note from Julie. My wife will be waiting for me. It's been almost two weeks since I saw her last.

I board the plane and find the nearest seat to the front. My ass hits it and before the plane lifts off the tarmac my eyes close.

It's hard to know if someone else is on a plane with you when your eyes are closed. They don't open up again until two hours later, and not even then until an attendant shakes my shoulder. I must say, the tumble of her blonde hair is impressive, along with her striking blue eyes. All that and a military uniform as well. Enough rank symbols have been flashed in front of my eyes for me to know she's a captain.

"Doctor, we're about to land." She stops shaking me as my eyes open.

"Okay," I yawn. "Is there any coffee, Captain..."

"Jesper. Sorry, I don't drink coffee, and I don't think you'd like to drink what would pass for my coffee."

We hit turbulence and she moves quickly to the seat across the aisle. Her hands fumble with the belt before it snaps into place. With a tug, she tightens it.

"Fly much?" I ask. Her face is ashen.

"Last time I did we dumped into the Pacific." Her hands are straining on the armrest.

"How long ago?"

"Four years, eight months, and twenty days ago."

"You keep count?"

"It's the last time I flew." She has an air sickness bag in her hand now.

I look around the plane. No one else is on board. "You're doing okay. We'll make it."

"That's what the pilot said. We'll make it. Next thing I know I'm shooting out of the cockpit with a rocket blasting me into the air. Do you know how cold the water is right after a spring melt? I do." Turbulence rock the plane.

The intercom comes to life. "We're landing in ten minutes. Fast approach protocol is approved. Please tighten your belts." The intercom snaps off.

"Fast approach?" I ask. Her eyes are closed now.

"Means we're aimed at the runway. He's going to burn off the altitude soon, take us right into the airport." She vomits into the bag.

The whine of the engines subsides and the plane's nose dips. A small TV on the bulkhead reads out the altitude and air speed. One is decreasing and the other is increasing. My stomach tries to climb out though my nose.

"In front of you."

I look over. She's holding another air sickness bag and pointing to the flap in front of her. "I'm not there yet."

We start levelling off, and a rumble shakes the plane as landing gear drops from the metal belly. My hands are now gripping the arm rests. The nose is up, the rear tires hit. It's the worst sound in the world, the sound of tires ripping across asphalt faster than they should be.

The sun is rising. Gold reflects off the tower's glass.

Once we're at the terminal, they rush us off the plane and through a blocked off section of security. It's the fastest I've been in and out of any airport. And before I know it, Captain Jesper has me by the elbow, moving us out to a waiting car. My bags are there. My wife is there. She rushes towards me.

She's in my arms before I know what's happening. The bear hug almost cracks my ribs. Her voice breaks the silence.

"I've missed you."

We lean in together. Lips meet.

Jesper clears her throat. "That's sweet."

I pull back and look into my wife's eyes. "I have a lot of meetings to go to, and the first one's in twenty minutes."

"Yes, I know. They told me. We get to catch up."

"Doctor, I've been assigned as your liaison with the brass," Captain Jesper says.

"Who are you?" My wife is looking over my shoulder.

"Captain Beatrice Jesper, you can call me Bes."

I'm surprised. "Beatrice?"

"You can call me Captain Jesper," she says, looking at me.

"Hi, Bes. I'm—"

"Sarah Fergus. Age thirty-seven. Doctorate in abnormal, cognitive and social psychology."

"You know a lot about me, it seems."

I turn towards the captain. "Well, if you must come with us…"

She nods and we all climb into the vehicle.

The driver gets us on the highway, then to the military base. Sarah has never liked fast moving vehicles. She tries to keep her eyes on me, but they wander to the road. I just try and hold onto her attention while lead foot moves us through traffic. Ten minutes later, we're pulling into the base, and it's guarded like Fort Knox.

Medals is waiting for us. He's wearing even more ribbons and dangling icons than the last time I saw him. Maybe a bus worth this time. Not one of them appears to be from combat.

The smile is plastic, his hand limp. My opinion of him is dropping by the moment. His badge hangs from the coat pocket. Billington, William. He's a General.

Jesper gets that ramrod look going as she salutes. Billington returns it with a limp hand. Sloppy. He reeks of stale cigar smoke and scotch. Must be nice.

Sarah takes the man's hand and I can see she's profiling him. Calculating eyes smile as her hand drops to remove his form her elbow.

"Welcome to Washington, doc."

"I have a lot of work to do. It would have been better to just come to the facility." Something tells me this man doesn't go anywhere for anyone.

"You live here, and so does your wife."

"We could have given her clearance to join me. Actually, that's a good idea. I want her to have clearance."

He smiles. "That's why she's here."

Sarah looks at me. "What's this all about?"

Billington puts his finger to his lips. "Not until you sign some papers."

I nod.

He leads us into the building, past more armed guards.

"They're a little paranoid here," Sarah says.

"You have no idea," I whisper back.

Into another office and we are directed to sit. Jesper just stands here, ramrod straight. A couple of MPs come in and take Sarah away. Billington tells me he'll make sure the interview goes well and to stay here. He leaves.

Jesper relaxes and looks at me. I shake my head.

"You do that a lot," she says.

"What?"

"Shake your head."

The statement bounces around in my skull. "I think it's better to shake my head than his." I cross my eyes. A little trick inherited from an aunt.

That gets me a smile.

"Do you report to him directly?"

She walks over to the chair next to mine. "No, thank God. I almost choke when his booze soaked breath hits me. He doesn't own a toothbrush from what I hear."

I chuckle.

"Did he earn all those medals or are they just for show?"

"Earned them, as far as being able to wear them. Most are from just being safe at the base when others went out to fight. All he had to do was be there for two weeks."

"And he gets a medal?"

"Ya, he gets a medal. Most soldiers don't wear theirs, but he does. All of them."

It's chitchat. We keep talking for a while, exchanging antidotes. I tell her how Sarah and I met, she tells me about her cats. Thirty minutes go by and Sarah comes back into the room, shaking.

She sits beside me and Jesper shoots up as booze breath comes into the room.

"She's legal," he says.

"You okay?" I take her hand.

A tear is in her eye.

"I-I can't believe it."

I reach for her hand.

"We have a few things to talk about." Billington sits behind the desk. "Jesper, relax."

"Yes, Sir."

"So, your supercomputer's not that super. Fudged the time frame by a month."

"With all due respect, General. Big Ben only had two hours of data to examine. Not much to tell the velocity of the 42, let alone know it was accelerating."

He nods. "Okay, doc. I'll give you that one. Are the ships ready?"

"No."

"Ships?" Sarah asks.

"There's a number of things not covered in the briefing, Mrs. Fergus."

"Project 'Out There' has five spaceships in the final stages of completion. We've been trying to finish everything off over the last few weeks." Sarah is staring at me. "Each will carry five hundred men and women to Gliese G. Everyone will be in suspended animation."

"And you've been involved in this for how long?"

"Only the two weeks." She squeezes my hand.

"How far?" she asks.

"20 light years. Gliese is in the constellation of Libra. Gliese G is in the zone."

Her eyes widen. "The Goldilocks Zone."

"We don't call it that. The habitable zone. Anyway, there are three planets that could sustain us, and it all depends on what we find when we get there. If we get there."

"What will stop us?" Sarah asks.

"Experimental drive systems, radiation, suspended animation, the unknown. Lots of issues. Hell, this is all a crap shoot anyway."

"But we'll survive." She is full of hope, anyone can see it. I'm no longer smiling, neither is Billington. Sarah is looking between the two of us. "We'll survive. Right?"

"The strongest have been picked for the trip," Billington says. "Couples in the right age and demeanour. All of them strong and capable of surviving off the land."

Sarah turns to me. "We'll survive. Right?"

A lump forms in my throat. I force a swallow and look down at the ground. "The human race will survive." My eyes meet Sarah's. "But we're too old to be picked for the flight."

Job Well Done

Two months have spun past so fast. We finally got the last of the ships ready. All the couples are now safe in suspended animation pods. Our five ships, all powered up and ready to go, sit upon the rail system. We'll get them up to Mach five before the chemical rockets ignite.

We're cutting it close. Only one week left. The 42 is visible in the sky now, both day and night. It was visible about two weeks ago, and the night Sarah saw it, she took her own life. No note. Nothing. She was living at the facility when it happened. I came home to our billet and her feet swung a foot off the ground. Tears streaked my face for a long time. Julie found me the next day, holding Sarah and rocking back and forth.

She helped me. Cleaned me up. Got Sarah ready for the MPs. We buried her at the base of the rail system. Jesper was there, along with Carl and Billington. The service took thirty minutes and we returned to work.

The countdown hits three and the power going through the rail shakes the whole countryside. Black smoke is pouring out of the fifty generators built on the site. Just enough power is generated to get the ships moving and keep the lights on.

My stomach flips as the five ships start moving down the ten kilometres of rail. At the end, the chemical rockets ignite and the ships arch to the heavens. Cheering rises from the control room.

We watch as the ships make their way out of the atmosphere, connect with the main drive systems in orbit and flush the first ton of hydrogen to accelerate. I say a silent prayer.

Two months. That's all it took us. Over a thousand technicians, welders, electricians and programmers have made it possible.

Hubble tracks the ships as they speed away. Their image becomes fuzzy as their speed passes the fastest man has ever gone before. Then nothing. No light is traveling fast enough to bounce off them. They have hit light speed.

Humanity has reached the stars. Hopefully, we will survive.

THE UNBOUND ANTHOLOGIES

MORE BOOKS PUBLISHED BY US

Winterbourne

Faun Song

The Spear Series

Escaping the Caves

Broken Star

Inside My Mind Volume I and II

Familiar Scents

Somewhere Beyond the Fire

The Elmnas Chronicles

Come to https://scififantasypublications.com for more on these amazing books